Inspect

John Gano was educated at Eton and Cambridge, where he read law with a particular interest in Criminology. He lives with his youngest son and daughter.

John Gano

Inspector Proby's Weekend

This edition published in Great Britain in 1999 by
Allison & Busby Limited
114 New Cavendish Street
London W1M 7FD
http://www.allisonandbusby.ltd.uk

First published by Macmillan Publishers Ltd, 1996

A catalogue record for this book is available
from the British Library

ISBN 0 7490 0418 5

Printed and bound by Biddles Limited,
Guildford, Surrey.

Chapter 1

'She shot him!'

Ted Rootham, still a detective sergeant at the age of thirty-two, stared at the big rumpled man sitting opposite. The atmosphere in the room had suddenly changed. There was an uneasy tension between them all, now that the words had been spoken. 'In the Library, you say?'

A jag of lightning flickered eerily through the half-closed curtains. 'I do!' said Proby, noting the anxious look on the face of the blonde woman sitting hunched between them. His wife no less.

'That's only a suspicion, Jim –' The noise of the thunder was shocking, intrusive.

'On the contrary,' snapped Proby, his grey eyes crinkled in victory, 'it's an accusation!'

'But …' Mollie Rootham, a nervous wisp of a creature beside the other three, was frowning. 'I still don't see …'

'Anyone contradicting me?' Proby leant forward and opened the envelope. 'There you are! Miss Scarlet, in the Library, with the revolver! He laid the cards down on the table with a satisfied snap. 'Who'd like some more coffee?'

This was a ritual, their Thursday evenings together, two couples who'd been friends for nearly ten years. Once they'd played whist, then canasta. Now it was the turn of Cluedo. Of the three this had proved the least likely to generate argument.

'Is it still raining?' Sheila Proby, svelte, voluptuous, raised her cup to accept her husband's offer.

'Pouring!' He didn't need to open the curtains. He could hear the water beating down on the roof of their new conservatory. He padded over to the kitchen hatch and came back with the coffee pot.

'This is *good*!' sighed Mollie. 'The real thing. No, just plain!' She watched her figure obsessively, a trim little woman with matchstick legs who could hardly look at Sheila's curves without revulsion. And yet it was Sheila who caused all the gossip.

'One more?' Proby was gathering the cards.

'I like this game,' said Mollie suddenly. 'The Ballroom, candlesticks. It's nice!'

'Certainly makes a change from the Willows estate,' said Rootham, smoothing his moustache. 'There you get the Front Room and a rusty cutthroat razor; and that's your lot. Listen to that thunder!'

Another shattering crash had shaken the house and then came the unmistakable clatter of a dustbin lid rolling across the back yard. As if that wasn't enough, the telephone began to ring.

'Yes?' Sheila was nearest, and handed it to her husband.

He listened for a moment. 'We're on our way. Ted Rootham was already up and making for the door 'Seventeen, Nevile Street!'

'Jim!'

'What?' Proby, who was pulling on an overcoat, stopped briefly to look down at his wife.

'Be careful!'

'Christ!' The rain was blowing horizontally into their faces, seeking and finding gaps in their clothing. When Rootham reached his car and opened the driver's door, it was nearly wrenched off its hinges by the gale. 'Who'd ever choose to be out on a night like this?'

'Silent alarm. One of ours. Turn here, and right at the end of the street!'

'Nevile Street? Above the jeweller's?' Proby nodded as their wheels skidded on the slippery tarmac. 'That's the *third* time.'

'So now … maybe …' Proby switched channels on the car-phone. 'Give us four minutes,' was all he said.

There'd be weeks, sometimes even months, when life for a detective in the rural city of Hampton could seem delightfully quiet. A few break-ins up in the Willows where the chief suspects were always the folk next door; a video here, a microwave there, or, outside the city, perhaps a few sheep or a garden mower missing out on one of the marsh farms further up the estuary. It was often more a question of paperwork than of serious mainstream crime.

But now, since the end of January, they'd had seven serious break-ins in five weeks, including an attempt on the Jewgate branch of Barclays Bank. And Dean and Dennis, the jewellers' in Nevile Street, had been raided two nights running, hence the fitting of one of his squad's own early-warning devices.

'You think it's the same lot?'

'Bound to be. Here we are.' And through the storm they could see another unmarked car reversing to block the side road: DC Allan, his face shockingly lit up by a brilliant flash of lightning, with a uniformed man already running up the street in the lea of a tall brick wall.

'I suppose he knows to wait?'

Proby's answer was lost in another great thunderclap. The storm must have been directly overhead. He ran round the corner, to find three men huddled in the jewellers' doorway.

'Who's got the back?'

'Skinner and Thompson.' They were talking in whispers. There was no light in the shop, nor in the flat above.

'Roof?'

'Oates is in number fifteen, and Allan's gone round the other way.'

'The back roads?'

'All blocked.'

'Open it up then.' If he was absolutely honest, this was more to his taste than Cluedo, even at the age of fifty-five. The dryness in his throat, the thrill of the dark, the camaraderie of his team, it was all worth a great deal more than any promotion, even though his feet were soaking.

'It's not locked!' It was true. The side door to the flat where the manager lived with his family just swung open to their touch.

'Slowly now.' Proby, using a pencil torch, edged into the narrow hallway. Absolute silence, apart from the eternal rain. He gestured to Rootham, who'd produced a formidable truncheon from somewhere. Cautiously they started up the shadowy stairs.

The first flight had only ten steps up to a landing where they had a choice: another short flight to the left led to a strong-room where the jewellers kept their stock, while that to the right continued up to the manager's flat.

'... ?' Rootham gestured to the latter with raised eyebrows. Proby nodded and again, very delicately for two heavy men, they edged up towards a flimsy deal door with grey glass panels. There was an enamel plaque which announced: '*Jane and Rico live here*', and someone had scrawled below, in red crayon, '*And Jemima*'.

This door was also ajar.

They looked at each other; both perfectly understanding the other's intentions. They could hear the other men creaking up the lower stairs now.

Rootham pushed the door; very gently, with his truncheon and then they were inside, Proby stumbling over something soft, a woman's body lying half under a table. He felt her squirm under his touch. At least she was still alive, her anguished face lit up by his torch, though mostly obscured by pink sticking-plaster. Her hair was matted with blood.

There were three doors from the hallway and he pointed silently to the first. Rootham charged through and was back in ten seconds, ready for the next. Within three minutes they had established that the intruders had gone. Rico himself was unconscious, tied to a chair in the kitchen.

It was Proby who found the little girl, crouched in her bedroom cupboard, hugging a small red leather suitcase. She couldn't have been more than six.

'Hello,' he said, squatting down beside her 'It's Jemima, isn't it?'

She stared up at him, her face rigid, betraying no expression of any sort.

'Your mum and dad are safe,' he said, pulling up his bedraggled socks, and trying to look less than his bulk. 'I like that suitcase. Is it yours?'

She nodded, and tears began to run down her face.

'I'm a policeman,' he said. 'My friends call me Jim.' She said nothing. She had gone very pale. 'The nasty men have gone ...'

She just stared. Then, in a small hard voice, '*Have they killed my daddy*?'

Proby put out a reassuring hand, ready to withdraw it if necessary. 'No,' he said, very gently. 'Your daddy's fine.'

She leant against his arm, looking up for and evidently finding something in his face that comforted her.

'That's good.'

The room was full of people now, and he handed her over to a policewoman who immediately wrapped her in a tartan rug.

'They never got as far as the strong-room.' DC Allan, trim and soft-footed, hardly looking old enough to shave, had been taking notes from the dazed manager. 'Three men, and maybe a woman.'

'Dressed?'

'Uniformed police!' Allan started to grin, saw Proby's face and abruptly assumed a serious expression.

'Bastards.'

'Dr Milligan says the woman's got a fractured skull. But he says she should be okay. That's the ambulance for her now.'

'The man?'

'A black eye, two teeth missing, otherwise fine.'

'So how ...?'

'Skinner ran into two of them in the back alley!' It was Rootham, his face dark with anger.

'And?'

'They bawled him out for taking so long to get there. One was dressed up as a chief superintendent.'

'That should have told him something was wrong!' muttered Proby. 'Description?'

'Nothing useful. Peaked cap, two eyes, a nose and a mouth.'

'That narrows the field.'

Chapter 2

'My dear James! The Chief Constable was in a sunny mood despite the previous night's débâcle. 'Such *bad luck*.'

Proby preserved his expression of polite enquiry. Between his kind of policing and that of his chief yawned an unbridgeable abyss. 'I spoke to the hospital this morning,' he said. 'The little girl should be fine.'

'Good! Excellent!'

'The mother's still on the critical list.'

'Really?' It was obvious he couldn't care less. 'Now, I've had another call from Hatton Abbey.'

'Sir?' It was unfortunate that Proby's immediate boss, Detective Chief Superintendent Rankin, was on one of his all too frequent periods of leave.

'Sir Thomas Hatton, you know. I had spoken to Mr Rankin about it. They're worried about break-ins. Lady Hatton is very frail, poor thing. She's awfully upset. I said you'd arrange to keep an eye on the place. Nothing excessive ... perhaps a couple of men round the clock for a week or so.'

Proby said nothing. After all, what was there to say? The days when local grandees could call upon the police as automatic private watchdogs were over for all except, it seemed, the Chief. But then his strange social ambitions, a rich source of comedy among his subordinates, were at the root of this.

Property, that jealous god of the wealthy, was no longer being automatically accepted as ranking as high in police priority as people. If the choice had to be made between chasing some thug who'd mugged an old lady or sniffing after a missing Old Master, and with their new financial constraints such a choice probably did arise, Proby was glad to endorse the former.

The Police Committee budget was under pressure. Money was undeniably short. In the last year alone, they'd had to reduce their target establishment by seventeen officers to help fund a new helicopter for the Traffic Division.

'Well? Can you arrange that?' It was clearly not put as a question.

'It'll mean taking men off the jewellery job.'

The Chief's smile died away. 'Surely not.' He was no longer looking at Proby when he spoke, an advance warning of trouble. 'It's simply a question of marshalling your resources more effectively. You know, I can't *think* why Rankin's always away when I need him.' This last was delivered in a pettish tone, with his right hand smoothing back the gleaming silver hair. 'It does fall within your area, doesn't it? I mean, I *am* right about that, I suppose?'

The worst of it was, he *was* right, for the great park wall of Hatton Abbey, topped nowadays with a liberal sprinkling of sharp glass shards cemented onto the coping stones, ran along the northern shore of the estuary just five miles inland from the port for all that the Abbey's main gates were a good ten-mile drive round by the A690 towards Castlewick.

'Yes, sir.'

'That's all right then. Sir Thomas has been a good friend to us.'

'*Us*, sir?' He couldn't help himself.

'Yes! Us!' snapped the Chief, feeling sorely tried. 'This force. And me personally. He has a lot more influence than you might think. Things don't change as much as some people might like them to.' He glared at Proby. 'Three times we've had the Police Ball at Hatton Abbey, *and* he made damn sure Councillor Hennessy got replaced when he kicked up that fuss about our new computer. You'd be making a big mistake to under-estimate Sir Thomas. It's people like him ...'

Proby had had enough. 'I'll go out there myself,' he said, looking at his watch. 'In fact I'd better be going now. Traffic are putting out flood warnings for all the roads round Castlewick.'

'Damn weather! It never seems to stop,' said the Chief, staring out at the rain. 'I'm most grateful.'

Proby nodded and left the office, just managing to close the door softly behind him.

'*Sir Thomas*'! '*Her Ladyship*'! He'd had quite enough of all that as a child, delivering telegrams for his father, the village postmaster, up the hill to Goonby Castle. Yet he had liked Lord Farthingdale, a kindly old man with only one eye, who used to keep a tin of Murraymints on his desk, and always dressed up as Father Christmas for the village party. It was his wife they all hated, with her plummy condescension and –

'What on earth are you muttering about?'

Proby started, and found Chief Inspector White from Traffic walking beside him towards the lift. Even chief inspectors seemed to be getting younger these days. This man must be the same age as Rootham.

'Any news on our rivals?'

Proby stared. 'Rivals?'

'The "*boys in blue*"! I heard all about it in the canteen. I always have had difficulty telling villains and detectives apart. But now they're putting on the same uniforms as well ...!' Chuckling, he wheeled off into an office before Proby could reply.

'*Sir Thomas*'! Proby, still grumbling defiantly, took the lift down to the car park, and found his red Saab blocked in by a big Jaguar saloon which was being polished by no less than three officers. No shortage of money there, it seemed.

'Won't be a minute,' called out the nearest man. Proby simply shrugged. He was in no hurry.

Chapter 3

The city port of Hampton lay on both sides of the estuary of the River Ham, a dark deceptive river born from a thousand small tributaries trickling down from the northern hills. The Romans had built a bridge here, of which only eighteenth-century illustrations remained, but so had Isambard Kingdom Brunel, and it was from this latter construction, a massive essay in granite and iron, that Proby, peering through the driving rain, could see the swollen grey waters surging towards the Atlantic. The torrent was dotted with churning debris. One, two whole tree trunks were being swept westwards as he watched, along with what looked suspiciously like the body of a cow.

The warehouses on the northern shore were already lapped by flooding, and for all that it was midday in March, he and all the other drivers were using their headlights.

Nor was the flooding confined to the river banks. Five miles out through the flat wasteland towards Castlewick, he met an ambulance speeding back into town and then saw ahead blue flashing lights, the melancholy harbingers of disaster.

A car lay upside down in a ditch, attended by a small group of firemen, while other cars were parked on the verges, their occupants standing about, shocked and bare-headed in the rain.

'Need any help?' He recognized the policeman directing traffic as PC Skinner, the man who had bungled the night before.

'No, thank you, sir. Two dead, I'm afraid.' The young policeman looked white with strain. 'Just youngsters.'

'All clear ahead?'

The constable pursed his lips. 'The water's over the road at Tenby Bridge.'

'I'm only going as far as Hatton St Mary.'

'Here comes the lifting gear now.' In his mirror Proby could see another massive machine, in scarlet livery, nosing past the cars behind him. He half raised his hand in salute and drove on.

Presently the landscape to his right began to alter. Gone was the bedraggled marshland and occasional poor cottage. In their place a more prosperous scene presented itself, lush meadows, thick forestry and smart farmsteads, their woodwork picked out in what was, even in so dreary a light, a cheerful if uniform blue.

Then, as suddenly as this paradise had appeared, so also it abruptly disappeared behind a tall grey wall, which, ignoring the twists and turns of the road, marched with an Imperial hauteur straight across the subdued countryside until the road joined it again beside a village sign.

Hatton St Mary was a peaceful cluster of gothic estate cottages in grey stone picked out in the ubiquitous blue, grouped around a stout little Norman church. The main road veered left out of the village, but the eye was carried straight on by a narrow avenue of oaks culminating in a massive pair of stone gate pillars, heavily rusticated, and surmounted by carved stone lions. The double gates were open.

Hatton Abbey. Private Entrance, read a sign, while another below it added:

Tradesmen's Entrance. 2nd Left →.

Proby smiled, though it had more of the appearance of a snarl. '*Sir Thomas*'! Even then it looked as if he would be saved from this fruitless and infuriating journey, because the Abbey drive curved down past a lake which was very clearly spreading across the parkland and had already covered the road. He brought the car to a halt at the water's edge, half hoping that perhaps he had found an excuse to turn back. But even as he paused, a battered Land Rover appeared from the trees beyond, bumping cheerfully through the water without even slowing, and covering his window with its spray. Gingerly, he drove slowly forward, stopping to test his brakes the other side. It could only have been a few inches deep after all.

The house was enormous, fifty perhaps sixty feet high, of rich golden stone with two massive pillars stretching up from the curved stone staircase at their feet to the heavy balustrade above their heads. It was all precisely symmetrical, so perfect in fact that for a moment he had the impression of looking up at a giant's doll's house. There were no doors at ground level, just opaque windows with thick iron grilles. Still muttering, Proby climbed the curving steps, clutching his hat which the wind was threatening to blow across the low-lying park to the far horizon.

There were wooden doors on the same scale, but these were fastened back, revealing a tall glass partition of many panes to match the flanking windows. A lower part of this evidently functioned as a door, for through it he could make out a shadowy figure indoors moving soundlessly towards him, its shape distorted by the glass.

'Sir Thomas?' He had decided to try to be civil.

'Who shall I say, sir?' The man had a blank face, pale and expressionless, though with thick red lips and a bald dome of a head, its sides wreathed with close black curls in the approved style of ancient Rome. His voice was sibilant, low and insinuating, and he carefully avoided Proby's gaze.

'Inspector Proby, Hampton CID.' Could this really be that creature of myth, the *butler*? If so, Proby was entirely prepared to believe in his guilt.

'Follow me, please.' The hall was a long gallery, tall and dark, opening on the left first into a high chamber hung with tapestries and then, shockingly, into a broad staircase, lit from behind by a massive window which must have risen the full height of the roof, some forty feet or more and so presenting a colossal and unexpected panel of pure light. 'Sir Thomas is expecting you.'

They had reached the other side of the house where more tall glass doors showed out onto a misty vista of topiary, fountains and, in the far distance, the rectangular glint of a strategically positioned canal.

'In here.'

Proby was not sure what he was expecting, a giant, perhaps, to match the masonry. He certainly had not expected the man who rose from behind a desk, a man who was barely taller standing up than he had been when sitting down.

'Inspector Proby?'

'Good morning, Sir Thomas.' The only sound in the room was the steady magisterial ticking of a heavy brass clock, itself four feet high and mounted on a gilt and tortoiseshell bracket fixed on the wall behind.

'A glass of champagne?' If the butler looked like Nero, this was Julius Caesar himself! Strong nose, hooded grey eyes, a firm uncompromising mouth, and a jutting jaw, yet almost a dwarf. He did not extend a hand but returned to his seat. Julius Caesar grown old, having survived the Ides of March. From the look of his skin, he must be late seventies, even early eighties.

'No, thank you, sir.' Dare he ask for tea?

'I hope you'll forgive me if I have one. I find it relaxes me.' He gestured to a chair.

Proby sat down, and decided against asking for tea. 'The Chief Constable said that you were worried about break-ins?'

There was a movement behind him. Another manservant! This one had brought the glass of champagne. He looked distinctly nervous.

'Thank you, Edward.' The little man took the glass and sipped at it thoughtfully. 'I don't expect,' he said, turning his basilisk stare back to Proby, 'that you will be altogether happy about being sent out here when you have so much to do in the city.'

Proby met his reflective gaze with a polite smile. 'The Chief Constable was very keen to oblige you, Sir Thomas.'

'No doubt.' The baronet allowed himself a brief, ironic smile. 'But I don't think I'm wasting your time. Do you believe in Evil?'

Proby's heart sank. Another nutter! Table-turning, the after-life, *voices* even. What it must be to have nothing to worry about except the fourth dimension.

'I see you don't. But then perhaps you see too much of it to grant it a separate existence?' He took another sip. 'My wife, who is very delicate in other respects, has a very healthy nose for evil. It is she who believes there is something wrong here. Something that needs to be prevented.' For a moment Proby thought he had caught a fleeting glimpse of an inner man, a hint of fear. Then the hard stare returned. There was something about his complete composure, his quiet lack of humility or self-doubt, that made him seem so formidable that his height became irrelevant. Perhaps that was the result of being very rich?

'The Chief Constable has asked me to keep a watch on the house. Have you had any sign of an attempted break-in?'

'*Burglars*, you mean?' Unexpectedly he laughed.

'It's always possible. We have a few good pieces here. Nevertheless, most of our losses tend to have been self-induced.'

Proby raised his eyebrows, confused.

'Well, for example,' said his host, 'the statues from the roof are in a museum. Even the big Rubens is in

Trafalgar Square now. People living in exaggerated houses tend to spend in an exaggerated way.' Again the hooded granite smile. 'Then they have to sell something. All bills have to be paid in the end, one way or another.'

'I see,' said Proby. Why the hell must Rankin be on holiday? This was just his sort of territory. He'd have positively enjoyed a good natter about old Rubens! The tall brass clock struck the quarter-hour, with a single clear note.

'I'll be grateful for anything you feel able to arrange.' With a shock, Proby realized the old man was standing up again, yet the great head had hardly moved. He was being dismissed. There must have been some invisible signal, for Nero was back, his red lips clamped firmly together and his eyes fixed on the floor 'My secretary, Miss Weissweiller, will make any arrangements you need.' The head turned away.

Proby stolidly followed the butler back towards the front door. The impression of noiselessness had not been an illusion. The man's progress was completely silent across the marble floor.

As they passed the foot of the great staircase, Proby had the fleeting but definite impression of a woman, frail and motionless, watching him intently from the high distant landing, silhouetted by the stormy yellowish light streaming through the immense window behind and above her. But whoever it was, it wasn't Lady Hatton, for just before they reached the door the butler turned smartly left through a low wooden door and called out, 'I have the *policeman* here, m'lady.'

'Who?' She had a low, husky voice, with a strong American accent. 'Why thank you, Maurice.' She was perched on a fragile sofa beside the tall fireplace of what in every other respect was furnished as a conventional dining-room. Proby stared down at her. She was even smaller than her husband, a tiny woman, but with a full figure and rounded, chubby features despite her age, which he put at seventy or more. Everything about her was still, almost creepily so. Except her hands. For all the frozen immobility of her face and body, her fingers were busily engaged in a frenetic nerve-wracked tattoo.

The butler seemed temporarily to have lost his composure. 'Inspector ... um ...'

'Proby.' He held out his hand, which she took with a quick trusting movement. Her grasp was cool, and just very slightly tremulous.

'Won't you sit down, just for a moment?' Her eyes were green, with long lashes, and distinctly oval in shape.

'Thank you.' The pink and gold sofa creaked beneath his weight. 'We're going to keep a watch here.' he said. She smiled. It was an oddly sad, even derisive smile. 'You'll be quite safe.'

'Poor Tommy,' she murmured.

'I'm sorry?' She was still holding his hand, but now she let go and her fingers resumed their ceaseless dance.

'He thinks money can solve anything. Servants, policemen, central heating!' She let out a low chuckle. 'Life's more complicated than he thinks.' Proby said nothing. To be truthful, he was rather offended. Yet wasn't this the very attitude he had expected? 'You try your best. But in the end, you can't change human nature. Wouldn't you agree with that, Mr Proby?' There was something almost vivacious in the way she cocked her head. Perhaps she was younger than he had first thought. Her face, though lined, retained a certain lustre. Yet the backs of her hands were withered, and covered in liver spots.

'My men will keep a good watch over you,' he said, feeling pompous and helpless both at the same time.

Again the strange deep chuckle. 'It's too late,' she said, adding quickly on seeing his expression, 'oh, it's not your fault, my dear. It's been too late for years.' She saw him staring at her hands. 'I used to be a concert pianist,' she said. 'Or could have been.' The green eyes disappeared momentarily as she blinked.

'Why did you give it up?'

'For *this.*' There was something indefinable in her words. It could have been a sneer, or a boast, but it was neither. Perhaps it was just a simple explanation, made complex for Proby by her unfamiliar accent and slow, reflective drawl. 'I played twice with the 'Frisco Conservatoire.'

'Really?'

'Yes.' She smiled shyly up at him. 'Mozart's 18th piano concerto and Beethoven's 3rd. They came to Belmont for my birthday.'

Suddenly her face lost all its animation and she seemed to sink away from him into the furthest corner of the little settee, becoming no more animate than one of the plumper cushions. Except for her hands.

'I will show you out, sir.' He'd quite forgotten the butler, Maurice, was still in the room with them.

Silently he led the Inspector back into the hall and out to the head of the outside stone staircase. When Proby, after a pause, turned to speak, the man had stepped back behind the glass partition. He heard the key turned decisively against further intrusion.

Chapter 4

Even though the rain had temporarily stopped, the floods were spreading. The water on the drive was deeper; and there was water, too, across the road in the village of Hatton St Mary.

Of the road accident, however, there was now no trace. Even the wrecked car had been removed, leaving nothing to tell that two young lives had been tragically cut short.

And he was being ordered to post a twenty-four-hour picket against '*evil*'! Two middle-aged men in mackintoshes pitched into an arena where the whole might of the Church Militant had, for two millennia, so conspicuously failed to deliver.

What was more, the centre of all this attention had told him herself that it was too late. Today was Wednesday, so they'd have a whole weekend of overtime to chalk up against the Chief's obsession with county society. He decided to call in at the hospital to see how Jemima and her mother were getting on.

Jane was still under sedation, and, peering through the glass, he caught just a glimpse of Jemima, her frail defeated figure slumped in a chair by her mother's bedside. As a young man leaving school, he had, thanks to an uncle who worked as a prison chaplain in Darlington, been fiercely in favour of the concept of justice tempered with mercy, improving prison conditions, shorter sentences, rehabilitation hostels. In fact that was what had first brought him to join the police, a wish to contribute, however indirectly, to the humane containment of crime. After thirty years of dealing with criminals, it was sights such as this, a mother and child shattered by casual greed, that made him shake his head at his former enthusiasms.

After that he drove back to his office. The three men had finished polishing the Jaguar and were now busily sponging down its interior.

With Rankin away, he had a full week's work just in dealing with his in-tray. There were reports to file, overtime and expenses chits to counter-sign, assessments to check and, worst of all, a new rota to be worked out for the division's reduced establishment. This was why he had always refused promotion, to *avoid* all this paperwork, yet here he was doing it anyway. Rootham was out following a lead about last night's crime, a delivery van spotted nearby with the last two digits of its registration as potential identification. Young Braithwaite was checking on the alibis of target suspects. In short the whole squad was out doing something useful, while he was cooped up in a grey plastic office, shifting *paper.*

What sort of villain carried out a burglary dressed as a chief superintendent? It was bizarre, and, he had to admit, ingenious. And, as it had turned out, effective. He rang down to the Computer Room to ask someone to run the idea through 'known methods of operation'.

Criminals, like policemen, tend to run in grooves. He lit a cigarette and inhaled the soothing familiar fumes of old tar. They'd fractured the mother's skull. Having broken in for the third night running. That sounded more like beginners. Maybe he should run a check on recently released juveniles?

He was still musing on the case when he was roused by the familiar sounds of his colleagues going home, cheerful voices in the corridor, slammed doors. And he'd made no progress with the paperwork after all. He was just piling it guiltily back into the tray when he remembered the Chief Constable and his particular problem, so the last thing he did before going home was to summon Allan and Oates and send them out to Hatton Abbey.

'What are we after, bloody poachers?' demanded

Allan, who had been looking forward to a night in with his wife and newborn daughter.

'Evil,' said Proby heavily. 'Evil's what they're worried about. Lady Hatton's had a premonition.'

'You serious?'

'Well, I'll let you into a secret,' said Proby. 'The Chief is. So keep on your toes. I'll send two more lads to replace you around noon tomorrow so you'd best take some food.'

'Why can't they feed us there?' growled Oates in a mutinous tone. Divisional darts champions weren't much amused by being deprived of a very necessary evening's practice before the annual competition.

'Because you're on watch. I want one of you in the car out of sight where the three drives converge. That way you can monitor any vehicles coming or going. The other one patrols the outside of the house. So take your raincoats and a couple of RTs so you can keep in touch. Call in hourly to the office. They'll keep me up to date.'

'You *are* serious!'

Proby bared his teeth. 'And don't ruffle their feathers. I don't want *Sir Thomas* calling the Chief Constable to say you weren't house-trained. Got it?'

The two men nodded gloomily and went out.

'I feel dreadful!'

It was so unlike his wife to complain. Proby gave her a sympathetic squeeze. 'Same place?' They were sitting together on the sofa, ready to watch a television serial they both enjoyed. The first thing she'd done on seeing him was to get him out of his sodden clothes and into a hot bath. Now, swathed in a dressing-gown she had warmed on a radiator; he felt agreeably drowsy.

'Mmm.' She nodded.

'Did you go to the surgery?'

She shook her head. 'I honestly didn't feel up to it.'

'Tell me where it hurts.'

She took his hand and placed it against her belly. Even her hand felt hot. 'I'm sure it's only indigestion.'

'Even so ...' He put one arm round her ample shoulder, pulling her against him. 'It's best to make sure.' She was, what, nearly forty? He must be getting old if he couldn't remember his own wife's age! But cancer, no less insidious an intruder than evil, calls for constant surveillance. '*Please*?'

She laid her head against his neck, and sighed. 'I'll go tomorrow. On my way to the shop.' Mondays, Wednesdays and Fridays were her working days, days spent sitting at the back of a small antiques shop in Northgate, while its proprietor, a trim young man, invariably dressed in pale tweed jackets over cavalry twills, combed the county for his stock-in-trade: Victorian clocks and barometers. He paid her five pounds an hour and five per cent commission if she sold anything. This in turn paid for their annual jaunt to a small hotel in Barbados. Such was their life, and so it had been, more or less, for over seventeen years.

Outside the rain had resumed, with interest. It was drumming on the roof, and beating against the windows. It had even seeped through under the front door; staining the carpet round the fitted mat. What must it be like for Oates and Allan, out there among those dripping bushes?

'What are you smiling about?'

He looked up at his wife's affectionate tone and hugged her closer. 'Nothing ... well ... Bill and Wayne are out on a wild goose chase tonight.'

'Those burglars?'

'You might well think so! No, they're out at Hatton Abbey, guarding our betters.'

'The place with the big wall? Does anyone still live there? I thought it was a hospital or something ...' She'd pressed the remote control so that a tiny red light blinked into life on the television.

'A very odd bunch ...' But her attention was on the programme now. They'd caught the end of the national news, with pictures of widespread flooding, two men drowned in Blackpool, train services disrupted on the East Coast line.

'Isn't that dreadful?' The Trent had burst its banks at Newark, and a bridge over the Tyne had been swept away near Hexham.

'We'll have problems here if the rain doesn't stop,' he muttered, his eyelids drooping. There was something about her proximity, the warmth of her lying against him, which often sent him to sleep now. It hadn't been like that when they first married!

'Come on ...' She was trying to lift him.

'What about the programme?' he murmured, resisting.

'I've taped it.' His head nodded against her. 'Come on! I can't manage you on my own ...' Wearily he let her help him to his feet.

Chapter 5

As soon as he woke, he knew something had changed. But what? It was certainly still raining. Then he realized. The room was colder than usual. It was also darker. The street lamp outside their window was no longer casting its familiar yellowish glare against the curtains. He stared at the window for what seemed an age. Then, gingerly disengaging himself from Sheila's outstretched arm, he slid out of bed. He froze as she gave a heavy sigh, turning over and wriggling against her pillow. But then her breathing returned to its heavy rhythm.

Relieved, he made his way cautiously round the foot of the bed, and gently moved the curtain. There was some little light from a sinister moon which seemed to be sailing high above dark stationary clouds. But the street itself was absolutely in darkness. No street lights, and, even odder, no light shining over Mrs Tate's door opposite. He felt the radiator. It was cold.

It didn't need long experience as a detective to deduce that the power must have failed. And surely not just in this suburb. Presumably the whole city was blacked out. Raising his eyebrows at the thought, Proby felt his way over to the door and pulled his thick tartan dressing-gown round his bare shoulders before very carefully opening the door. There was, of course, no light now in their hall either.

He walked downstairs and into the kitchen. Everything was dark, and when he lifted the telephone, the line was dead. So! With just the hint of a smile, for he was a man who thrived on drama, he unlocked the glass door that led to the garage and retrieved his mobile phone from the car. The noise of the rain was ceaseless, almost subliminal after all these weeks. He dialled the radio room number and got an engaged signal. Not surprising, he thought, and padded back to his desk to find the list of emergency numbers. The stain by the front door had spread another foot. He looked for the clock on the video, but that was dark too. And the one on the oven. Was the world too much in thrall to electricity? At least his wristwatch hadn't stopped. It was still lying where he had left it on the coffee table. 04.34 a.m. Glory be to God for clockwork things.

Winding it, he tried Radio Control and then the Stockard Street despatcher. Both engaged. He tried Rootham's personal RT and got an immediate ringing tone.

'Yes?'

'Ted?'

'What a mess!' Accompanied by a chuckle.

'Where are you?'

'Junction of Rupert Street and Coronation.'

'What? What are you doing there?'

'Coming to collect you. The telephone lines are all flooded. And you weren't answering your bleeper.' Proby suddenly had a guilty image of the offending device in the pocket of yesterday's sodden trousers, and them buried under a pile of laundry at the far end of the kitchen.

'What's up?'

'It's Oates. He called in forty minutes ago.'

'And?' Proby felt the familiar surge of adrenaline.

'Reception was very bad, but we got some of it. It's Lady Hatton. She's dead.'

It was eerie, driving through the darkened city. No traffic lights, few cars yet, and all around them the grim façades of unlighted buildings.

'The river's over in several places,' said Rootham. 'But it beats me how the Telecom people didn't take precautions.'

'How long before they restore the service?' Even as he

asked, Proby realized the futility of his question. Of course teams would be working on it now. 'The bridge?'

Rootham chuckled. 'Sound as a bell! They knew how to build in those days.' He had to steer around a lorry, abandoned at the side of the road. At least its side-lights were still working. 'But Traffic Division say the main roads are all closed now.'

When they reached Police Headquarters, the seven-storey block at the top end of the inner ring road, everywhere was in organized chaos, with the emergency lighting casting austere shadows over uniformed men hurrying in all directions.

'Thanks for coming in!' It was White, the youthful Chief Inspector from Traffic. 'We need all the help we can get.'

'Going straight up to the top floor,' said Proby, with a kindly show of regret. 'Possible job of our own. But,' he added, seeing the other man's face fall, 'if it's a false alarm, I'll gladly come and muck in.'

'You do that,' said the other. 'Half the reserves are out of contact. I've even got the Chief's driver out directing traffic down by the docks.'

'It *must* be serious then,' said Rootham, and the two detectives stepped into the lift, leaving their colleague smiling wryly.

'You see?' The Chief Constable was in his element preparing to take a call from the Home Office via the radio link with one hand, while directing the strategic placing of coloured pins on a county map with the other 'There, Dorothy! And there, by the Cathedral! Now, tell me what's happened at Hatton?'

'We've just had a single call sir,' explained Rootham. 'DC Oates rang in on his RT to say that Lady Hatton has been found dead. There was no specific mention of a *crime* . .'

'Didn't you ask, man?'

'The duty sergeant took the call, sir,' replied Rootham stolidly. 'There was a lot of static. We've been waiting for him to call back since. They tried to telephone the house, but of course the whole system had gone down by then. And the roads are all closed.'

'Well, I'm ahead of you there,' said the Chief smugly, with what almost qualified as a grin. 'Traffic's new toy is waiting for you at St Swithin's Comprehensive. Make it quick, because they've got a hundred and one other things to do after they've brought you back.'

'You mean ...' Proby risked a glance at Rootham.

'The helicopter, of course! Sir Thomas will be suitably impressed, I think. Off you go!' From the map, the Chief Constable's aide gave Proby an eloquent gesture of despair. Only she must know what anguish the diversion of their best means of rescuing people stranded by the floods to this indeterminate errand must be causing.

Seizing his excuse to leave, Proby turned abruptly and hurried down the corridor, with Rootham on shorter legs, scurrying behind. While Rootham collected their usual scene-of-crime bag, Proby foraged for a briefcase into which he crammed two torches with spare batteries, his office pullover, his own forensic kit and, as an afterthought, the sponge-bag he kept there for working overnight. It was only then that he remembered he'd not left a note for Sheila, to explain where he was going. She'd wake, in a cold dark house, to find herself alone, without explanation. He had already reached for his telephone before remembering that it would be dead. What a fool!

'Are we off?' Rootham stuck his head round the door. 'What about arms?'

'NO!' Proby was already tiring of this escapade. 'She probably had a heart attack.' Poor old woman. He'd been impressed by her fragile dignity and evident simple niceness. In fact he was feeling a real sense of pain that she was dead, that those magnificent green eyes had lost their scope for ironic observation.

Rootham grinned. 'Especially if she saw Bill Oates peering at her in the undergrowth in the middle of the night!' Proby shook his head.

They rode down to the ground floor and paused by the front desk to check if any further message had come in from Oates or Allan. There was nothing.

'I thought you said you were going to help,' shouted White, coming up behind them.

'As soon as we can, sir,' said Proby.

'How can you justify commandeering my helicopter?' demanded the other man. 'I've got three cars stranded out by Tenby Sluice, and there's a report of people with children on the roof of a farmhouse down on the Marsh.' He was suddenly very red in the face.

'If it helps, sir,' said Proby calmly, 'I'd far rather be fetching them than following the Chief's wild goose trail.'

'It doesn't,' retorted White, shaking now. He must have been on duty for over twenty-four hours already, and it showed in his appearance. 'It doesn't help. Just bring that *fucking* helicopter back and quick!' He turned away. They watched him walk, unsteadily, back to the switchboard room.

'That one'll crack up if he doesn't take some rest,' muttered Rivers, the duty sergeant, who'd come over at the sound of a raised voice. 'People who drive themselves too hard are no good to anyone. You want a car to the chopper? I've got half an hour off I'll drive you down there myself.'

'Thanks,' said Proby. 'With any luck we'll be back here in an hour or so. Then we can give you a hand!'

It was a very short flight once the helicopter, vibrating noisily, had lifted them up above the school playing field and swooped effortlessly over the gasworks.

They crossed the river, the swollen grey torrent awash with debris. Its normal course was lost within the vast expanse of muddy water. Only the tops of trees and buildings showed where once-dry land had yielded to the flood. It wasn't a beautiful sight at all, but menacing, in the grey light, to see the cold remorseless advance of swirling water.

The line of the Hatton park wall far below them now seemed no more than an intermittent pencil line drawn on a map of water, then some smooth plantations on higher ground and now, in the half-light, they could see the house, isolated on its own small irregular island of garden. Its honey-coloured rectangular block, as high as it was wide, was more than ever like a doll's house, as it sat presiding over a geometrically satisfying composition of flower beds and shrubbery, though smudged now with the encircling flood. Nor had the water advanced uniformly. The forecourt, for example, was all dry, whereas the water was already near to lapping against the house's eastern wall.

Rootham shouted something above the blast of the rotors.

'WHAT?'

'I SAID, IT DOESN'T LOOK MUCH LIKE AN *ABBEY* TO ME.'

Proby looked away irritably. From above, he could see now that the high balustrade hid innumerable chimneys, some of them smoking busily, and above them a bedraggled flag, lacerated by the persistent gales.

Lady Hatton was dead. That much was certain. But people did die, even in palaces. Especially if they were over seventy.

He didn't like to admit, even to himself, that much of his anger was due to a fear of flying, especially in helicopters. The pilot was gesticulating at him. Why couldn't the bloody man keep his hands on the controls? Now he was pointing downwards. Surely the fool wasn't going to try to land on the roof?

He shook his head furiously, and was rewarded with a satirical smirk. Abruptly the machine banked, descending in a steep spiral and landing very softly, nose first, on the broad forecourt in a storm of dust and gravel.

The two detectives, clutching their bags, clambered out. The place seemed entirely deserted. There was a shout from the pilot.

'WHAT?' Proby could feel his question blowing away even as he shouted. The man was clutching his headphones and mouthing at them. 'I can't HEAR you!'

'... EXPLOSION ... RUFUS DOWN ATOMIC RESEARCH ... EMERG ...' The pilot's words were blown away among the scream of the helicopter engine and the rattle of its blades.

'WHAT EXPLOSION?' shouted back Rootham. 'What's he *talking* about?'

To their dismay the pilot made a gesture of giving up, pulled the door shut and immediately the machine rose a few feet into the air with a frightful clatter, hovered uncertainly for a moment, and then swept up and over the far wall and away into the sky, paler now with the approach of dawn.

'Bloody hell!' roared Rootham. 'I thought he was supposed to wait for us.'

'He was,' said Proby. 'He'll be back.'

'Not if they've got real bother up at Rufus Down. You wouldn't think a bit of rain would cause all this, in *England* of all places! Will you look at this dump? They've got no electrics here either.' Rootham shook his head in utter gloom.

It was true. As the dust settled, they could now see that several of the tall windows were lit from within by the soft guttering glow of candles, though most were still shuttered and dead.

'Thank God!' It was Allan, dirty and unshaven, looking more like a villain than a guardian angel.

'What's up then?'

'We couldn't telephone and the road's completely blocked.'

'Yes,' said Proby, feigning patience. 'But what has happened?'

'The old lady's dead.' He seemed in a strange mood, almost a trance.

'And?'

'You'd best see for yourself.' And he headed off up the exterior staircase, shaped like a horse-shoe which led to the front door.

'Good morning, Maurice.' The butler, immaculate as before, was standing silently inside. He inclined his head at Proby's greeting and closed the door behind them and locked and bolted it.

'I can see both doors from here,' he said suddenly. 'No one can come in or go out without my seeing them. Or Miss Fisk over there.'

Rootham and Proby stared at him and then at a shadowy figure seated on a gilt chair in the far corner.

'Thank you,' said Proby.

There were candles everywhere, tall ones, short ones, twisted and scented ones, all thrust into a wonderful variety of holders, ranging from single brass candlesticks to a solid gold candelabrum of tortured rococo design, glittering massively on a console table at the foot of the stairs. The hall looked, and smelled, like a church, with the high stone walls richly gilded by the flickering light. Beyond, however, lay caverns of darkness, as one archway followed another, retreating into a fathomless gloom.

He walked over to the seated figure, as square and motionless as a Buddha.

'Miss Fisk?'

'I am,' came the uncompromising reply. He could hardly see her in the shadows. 'Fine time this is to wake folks up.'

'I'm sorry.'

'Traipsing all over.' She sucked in her breath sharply. It sounded as if they hadn't told her what had happened.

'You've seen no one?'

'Course not.' Her gravelly voice brimmed with disdain. 'What would you expect?'

'Thank you,' he said, trying to disarm her with civility. She muttered something, which he couldn't make out, but which sounded as if he had failed. With a friendly nod, he moved back towards the others.

'This way ...' Allan was already climbing the first dark flight of stairs. The steps were stone and at least ten foot wide. Menacing shadows, purple and black, receded at the flash of their lamps. 'I don't know what went wrong with the radio.'

'Tell me about Lady Hatton ...'

'The batteries ... may ... have gone ... Bill ...' It was useless. He was almost inarticulate.

Up and up they climbed. These steps were almost as deep as they were broad, so that their progress, past faded wall frescoes on one side, and gilded iron balustrading on the other, seemed interminable. There were statues in niches too, pale and brooding, and there at the top, just as still, stood Edward, the other manservant, armed with a hurricane lamp, watching them impassively, to one side of a doorway which gave onto another gallery.

'Where's the Ballroom then?' whispered Rootham facetiously.

Proby ignored him. 'Lady Hatton?'

'This way.' Edward had turned ahead of them and was leading the procession down the left of a gallery that more than matched the one below in candlepower, until they reached a tall pair of double doors.

'In here, Inspector.' It was the first time he had heard Edward speak, a soft voice, with a nasty edge to it.

Lady Hatton's bedroom was very far from what Proby had expected. Despite its size, it was, if anything, more like a hospital room than a private apartment. A single bed, with metal sides, stood at a strange angle in one corner, and there was one armchair, also metal, beside a writing desk. The floor was bare, with polished boards, and high windows, uncurtained, were still shuttered against the storm outside. It was a bleak, sad room, and this impression was not softened by the body lying curled up beside the empty fireplace. Lady Hatton was naked, and dead. It was only when Proby knelt gently beside her that he could see that one side of her round little head was crushed. There was even a piece of bare skull showing through the matted hair.

'Not much blood,' he noted to Rootham, who had let out a soft whistle. 'She must have died instantly.'

'The weapon's next door.' He hadn't noticed Oates come in. He too looked shocked, and dirty beside the gleaming Edward. 'Let's see.' He rose and followed the constable through into a lower room, really more a corridor lined with deep cupboards. A divan, recently slept in, was placed in front of the window, and beside this, lying on the floor, was a heavy brass door-stop in the shape of a lion, freely moulded. One side of its base was discoloured and the carpet where it lay had a small brown stain. 'Bag it,' said Proby tersely to Rootham, who was already unpacking his brief-case, 'and cover the area with something non-absorbent. We'll have to seal both rooms until we can get some Forensic back-up.'

Returning to the body, he knelt down and tenderly lifted the dead woman's head, trying to remember everything he had picked up from observing Doc Milligan over the years.

The body was just beginning to show signs of stiffness. Given the room temperature, that meant she must have died, what, four to six hours ago? Between twelve-thirty and two-thirty in the morning? He smiled grimly at the thought of being cross-examined by an experienced defence counsel. He hadn't one qualification in the world, having left school at fifteen.

Lady Hatton had been such a small woman with well cared-for hands and feet. Apart from her crushed skull, she seemed in good order, though there was a bruise on her left ankle. It had bled a little, therefore it had been caused before death. A woollen pyjama jacket was hanging loose on one of the black firedogs in the hearth, and the matching trousers were sprawled across the bedhead. There was plenty of light now, as spiky sunbeams pierced the rain, making the candles redundant.

Risking the undying enmity of Forensic, and following a hunch, he made a quick but careful search over the rest of the floor, and was rewarded by three tiny bloodstains, one on the floorboard beside the writing desk, a similar one by the inner door and one on the foot of the angled bed. The only other thing he found was a tiny triangular chip of opaque glass, lying beside the stone hearth.

'What are you looking for?' Rootham more conventional in staying motionless in the doorway to avoid disturbing good evidence, had been watching him with a wry smile. Perhaps Proby had always secretly wanted to be Sherlock Holmes, super sleuth. On this occasion he had no choice.

'Confirmation.'

'Of?'

'How I think she died.'

'Give!'

'I think she knew the killer. I think he or she came at her with that door-stop, and I think she ran to the bed and pulled it to that angle as a means of blocking the pursuit. But the killer climbed over the bed, so she fled, banging her ankle against that caster on the foot of the bed. She ran towards the door but he cut her off, so she started flinging off her clothes, perhaps to try to distract him. Then maybe she slipped on the wood. He caught her by the fireplace and smashed her skull for her.'

The room was silent, the few pieces of furniture unable to refute or confirm this account of a terrified old lady's last moments. Proby and Rootham stared at each other, each thinking the same, as they often did. Lady Peacock, in the Bedroom, with a door-stop. Only here it wasn't a game. It was pitiful, and cruel, and it made them both very angry.

'Seal both rooms,' said Proby, and pulling the top sheet from the bed, in defiance of all rules of procedure, he laid it softly over the body. 'Let's get to work.'

There could be no doubt that they were dealing with murder. Nor that the murderer, confined by the floods, was still uncomfortably close at hand, somewhere indeed inside this very building.

Chapter 6

'Just like the old days!' They'd been given a room in the north-east corner of the house, on the main floor, reached by walking past the great staircase and then turning left through a low corridor past a service staircase and the ground-floor lavatories.

As an Incident Room, it left much to be desired. They had no computers, two battery-powered police radios in place of the usual banks of telephones, and just the four of them to do the job of twenty.

'Did you get through to Rivers?'

'Not really,' said Allan, shaking his head. 'Too much bloody static. I don't think he could hear me at all. I thought I'd try later with the new batteries. Failing that, I could try swimming if you think it's necessary. I want to get away from here.'

'We'll see. At the moment you're more valuable here. The pilot's bound to come back this afternoon anyway.'

The arrival of Proby and Rootham seemed to have restored the two junior detectives to something like normality. Allan, a stocky man with receding brown hair and close-set eyes, had been hit by a stomach upset shortly after their arrival on watch. Unwilling to face the occupants of so imposing a house, he had spent a wretched night commuting to and from a disused lavatory in the stables. Yet even from there he had had a clear view of the front courtyard. Oates, on the garden side, thin, wiry, built like a terrier under a thatch of unruly reddish hair, had, as usual, the quivering energy of one excited by the chase.

And of one thing they were both certain: without their knowledge no one could have entered or left the house before the alarm was raised, and no one could have left it since, with Maurice and two of the women servants taking it in turns so there were always two of them there. For one thing, the house had only those two doors, one each on the entrance and garden fronts, both on the raised main floor and reached by matching curved exterior steps. There were indeed windows giving onto the basement at ground level, but these were all solidly barred, both inside and out.

There was no other way in, or out. The murderer must, therefore, be among the occupants of the house.

'So let's hear the worst. How many are we dealing with?'

'More than you'd think,' grunted Allan, whose thoughts were mainly with his wife left on her own with their newborn baby, while he spent a windswept night nurse-maiding a horde of 'distressed gentlefolk' as he had sourly described his posting to Sergeant Rivers *en route* to collect the car from the pound. 'I've got a list here.'

Proby sat back in his chair. It was wooden, leather-padded, and it swivelled on three chunky oak legs. 'Let's hear them one by one, with your immediate impressions.'

Oates and Allan exchanged a quick nervous look. 'Some of them have never appeared ...' said Oates. 'I stayed with the body ...'

'And I stayed outside till I heard you coming to land,' added Allan.

'Okay, okay,' said Proby with a smile. 'Just tell us what you've got.'

'There's four in the family,' said Oates. 'That's Lady Hatton, who's dead. Neither of us met her at all.' He glanced at Allan, who nodded confirmation. 'Then there's Sir Thomas. Quite frankly he scares me stiff. No one's seen him since the body was discovered. Then there's the son, John, late forties, bit of a runt, affected, smokes those black cigarettes through a holder. And the daughter …' he glanced down at his notes. '… Emily, bit of a looker, thirties, appears very upset. I think she's with her father now.'

Rootham was writing it all down. 'Right?'

'Well, there's five "guests", or sort of –'

'Sort of?' snapped Proby, who was growing impatient.

'Unintentional guests, if you see what I mean. We got here at six, and had great difficulty getting through the water on the drive. Miss Clare, that's Miss Dolly Clare, lives in the village and tried to go home before dinner. Passed us on the way out. But she had to come back because the water on the drive was too deep. She's in her seventies, a good friend of Lady Hatton's. Like for fifty years.

'Then John Zeberdee Boyce, tall, big man, Sir Thomas's solicitor, lives in Castlewick. He'd been here all day, was invited to stay for dinner, and then had to stay on because of the road being blocked.

'Rupert Humphrey. Calls himself "Captain" so I suppose he's a regular soldier, or was. A friend of the son's, though he's younger, perhaps forty? He was staying here anyway. I get the impression they were in the army together.

'And then there's the Colonel, Colonel Fetherstonehaugh.'

'You serious?'

Oates grinned. 'Straight up. Not in the best of health, though. Emaciated. Bent. Eighties at least, smokes like a chimney. He is one very upset old gentleman.'

'And the fifth?'

The two detectives looked at each other 'Very pretty lady. Mrs Violet Roberts. I wouldn't like to guess her age. Very elegant. Lots of scent. Allan here thinks she's the son's floosie, but I'd put my money on the old bugger.'

'Sir Thomas?'

Oates nodded. 'I had a chance to look round some of the bedrooms when the servants were getting dressed. She keeps quite a wardrobe of clothes in an empty room next to Sir Thomas. I'd say she's his mistress. But she says she lives out towards Castlewick, the Old Manor House or some such address.'

'Servants?'

It was Allan's turn. 'There's the cook, Mrs Freeman, fifties, lives out with her husband in the lodge by the main gates but stayed in to nurse Nanny Fisk, who's very elderly, eighty-six-ish, very asthmatic.

'Miss Weissweiller, the secretary. Sixties. Pointy nose, eyes like gimlets. She looks straight through you, very sharp. If anyone here knows what's going on, it's her.

'Maurice Bourke, the butler. He's sixty-three. Been here forty-seven years. Started as pantry-boy in the late forties. Very evasive. But, and here's something more to the point, the other bod, "footman" or whatever he calls himself, Edward Drury, aged thirty-five, I'm certain is on our books. I know his face, and the way he reacted to us … he has form. I'm sure of that.'

'Thirteen people,' said Rootham, ticking them off. 'And Lady Hatton, poor old lady. Any comment about her being unclothed?'

The two detectives shook their heads. 'I'd say,' ventured Oates slowly, 'that that wasn't a surprise. Not to the servants, and not to her daughter. No one else has seen her.'

'Who found the body?'

'Mrs Freeman, the cook.'

'And who alerted you two?'

'No one. I heard the screams, and fetched Allan from the bog. He moved round to watch my side while I hammered on the front door till someone opened it.'

'Who was that?' asked Rootham reaching for a fresh pad.

'The butler. They just call him Maurice.'

'Dressed?'

'Looking like bloody Fred Astaire!'

'How long did you have to wait?'

Oates shrugged. 'Seven minutes? It seemed a lifetime. But there was no way we could break through that lot.'

'Sure someone couldn't have slipped out the door the other side?'

Allan shook his head again vigorously. 'I was round there at once,' he said. 'It was the first thing we thought of. Both doors were heavily shuttered. It takes them three minutes to shift all the bolts. And Maurice has the only keys.'

'Who says?'

'Maurice,' said Oates. 'Confirmed by Miss Weissweiller, the secretary. There is a second set, but he has them both on the same key-ring.'

There was a knock on the door, and Edward came in, carrying a tray loaded with cups, a pot of fresh coffee, even a plate of hot toast. 'Mrs Freeman thought you'd need this, sir,' he said, putting it down carefully on the desk. 'What time would you like breakfast? We're having a bit of a battle without any power.'

Proby rubbed the back of his head, feeling disoriented. 'That's kind,' he said, noting the other men's eagerness. 'I'd have thought you'd have a generator here. In case of emergencies.'

Edward shook his head. 'You'd need a small power station for a place this size. But the heating and hot water work off a solid fuel boiler, and we do have one calor-gas cooker. Mrs Freeman says she'll be sorted out very soon.'

Proby nodded. 'Fine. But first we need to search the house. It's almost seven o'clock,' he added, looking at his wrist-watch. 'Is everyone up?'

'I believe so, sir,' replied Edward, 'except Mrs Roberts. But I would expect her down within the next few minutes.'

'Then please ask Sir Thomas if everyone could be assembled somewhere suitable, so that we can start our search. Say in, what, ten minutes?'

'That will give you gentlemen time to drink your coffee,' said Edward pleasantly, and left them staring after him.

Hatton Abbey

GROUND FLOOR PLAN

GARDEN DOOR

FRONT DOOR

N

ROOMS:

1. Gallery
2. Dining Room
3. Pantry (+ lift)
4. Saloon
5. Library
6. Morning Room
7. Ante Room
8. Estate Office
9. Secretary
10. Justice Room
11. Trophy Room
12. Lavatories
13. Tapestry Hall

STAIRCASES:

A. The Great Staircase.
B. Back stairs to basement & 1st Floor
C. SE (red) stairs to mezzanine rooms
D. NE (blue) stairs to mezzanine rooms
E. Steps down to basement (NE & NW)

Chapter 7

The search revealed nothing that they did not already know. The thirteen people who waited awkwardly in the room they called the Saloon were the only occupants of the house, apart from the dead body, still lying where they had found it.

The main family and guest rooms all with ceilings nearly twenty feet high, were arranged on two floors on either side of the central galleries and reached via the great staircase. There were, however, three subsidiary staircases, each of which led to other rooms, low cramped chambers awkwardly lit by windows that either started at floor level or opened only by the ceiling, and there were five floors of these, ingeniously piled one upon the other in spaces not already filled by the high state rooms.

These smaller rooms were used by the servants and also, some years before, judging by the faded bears and peeling giraffes, by the children of this and previous generations of Hattons.

None of this made the search, with only four policemen, absolutely certain, but after two hours Proby was satisfied that he had explored the whole building, even the basement, reached only by the Back stairs, and also by two separate sets of stone steps in the northern two corners of the house. Down there they had found the kitchen, two pantries, a number of utility rooms (for laundry, storage and so on) and nothing else. They'd even searched the wine cellar. There was no one else there.

After one further look at the body he walked down the Back stairs which led directly to the entrance hall, and round through the Library and into the Saloon.

The atmosphere there was one of total gloom. He went straight up to Sir Thomas who, with a cashmere rug thrown over his knees, was sitting sipping tea in a wing chair by the empty fireplace.

'Good morning, Inspector.' The old man deliberately got his greeting in first.

'Good morning, Sir Thomas. I'm very sorry indeed.'

The heavy bald head inclined, fractionally. 'Let me introduce the people you haven't met. Mrs Frank Roberts ...' Oates had been right. She was beautiful, a tall, slim woman, nearing forty perhaps, but still blooming, with large grey eyes and glossy black hair cut short to the nape of her long neck. '... my daughter Emily ...' Another piece of fancy decoration, this one blonde, with rounded features reminiscent of her mother, full lips and a serpentine figure. He liked the way she held her head, the way her eyes met his, demure but somehow challenging. Proby forced himself to look away.

'... Miss Dolly Clare ...' A dumpy, wispy old lady, still in a pink silk peignoir, with an apple-cheeked complexion, pale blue eyes as big as saucers and fine fluffy white hair, very carefully combed. She caught the Inspector's eye and smiled vacantly, as if this were a social occasion.

'... our friend Colonel Alec Fetherstonehaugh ...' The old soldier was sitting opposite his host, in a matching wing chair. He had a rug too. Perhaps they spent every day copying each other? But this man was sick. His watery eyes were sunken into a flaccid freckled complexion, and only a few faded strands of hair covered a head long polished and discoloured by some alien sun. To be blunt, he looked like an ailing tortoise, with his wrinkled neck and slackly toothless jaw. He also appeared to be having a stroke. One side of his face twitched constantly, and whenever he raised his hand to take a deep pull at his cigarette, it shook violently. The ashtray beside him was already piled with stubs.

'... my son John ...' Proby tried not to stare. The son was barely taller than his father, an etiolated figure, immaculately over-dressed in a fine pale silk suit neatly buttoned over a fat black satin tie, obviously hastily borrowed, perhaps from one of the servants. His greeting was the momentary lowering of his eyelids, the barest flickering of good manners, before returning to the serious business of screwing a fresh cigarette into a long holder.

His eyes felt drawn again to the daughter. To his embarrassment he found she was staring back. Just thinking of looking at her was making his heart beat faster. He must pay attention! The old man's voice had changed note. '... er ... Captain ... um ... Humphrey.' Clearly the Captain was not an approved guest. Not was it surprising. The man was a monster to look at, especially for one comparatively young in that household, with a shiny bulging face, scarlet-veined cheeks, and a swollen sagging dewlap. He smirked at the Inspector and raised one hand in greeting from where he sprawled, very much at his ease, on a long sofa.

'Good morning to you, Inspector!' The second one actually to speak.

'... Mr John Boyce, our family lawyer ...' The old man's voice ground on, grimly ignoring the interruption, and indicating a tall heavily built man with grey hair slicked neatly back, consciously distinguished, who towered over his master yet managed, by the angle at which he presented his great bulk, to indicate where the power lay. He nodded abruptly to Proby. Had they met before? Or was it just a 'we professionals' acknowledgement?

'... Miss Fisk ...' The other sentry at the time they had arrived. An old battle-axe if ever he'd seen one, a squat old woman, densely made, in fact almost a cube, with a square bewhiskered jaw set like a bull-dog, and angry little eyes. She seemed to be daring him to blame her for anything.

'... my secretary, Miss Weissweiller ...' Allan's description has been spot on. A short trim woman, age indeterminate, with grey hair scraped ruthlessly back and a brisk air of impenetrable unemotional efficiency. She was wearing thick rimless spectacles, which flashed with aggression. He was suddenly sure that she minded the intrusion more than the crime. Again his eyes swivelled towards Emily. This time she smiled openly. He had an uneasy feeling that she knew exactly what he was thinking.

'... Maurice and Edward of course you know, but Mrs Freeman ...?' His voice tailed away, as if inspiration failed. Proby suddenly had a crisis of unreality. This was a nightmare! Surely soon he would wake up, find himself back in the street, among his own people, among the comfortable paraphernalia of Divisional back-up. Not here, almost alone, among all these strange creatures who were staring at him. Anyway, the cook was wrong. Surely she should have been a stout old party with a stage accent and phoney laugh, with about five minutes to live before being found, ready jointed, in her own deep freeze. Not this trim smart woman who was already signalling her desire to leave the room.

'May I?' Her voice was as cool as her appearance. 'I should be preparing breakfast. Your men have been out all night.'

A rebuke! Surely she must realize there was a job to be done? Listlessly, he nodded. 'Go ahead,' he said. 'I will interview you each in turn. My sergeant here will fetch you. In the meantime, I must ask you all not to leave the house.'

'What? No walkies in the pouring rain? That's not very healthy, Inspector.' Captain Humphrey was almost chortling. Perhaps he was drunk.

Proby decided to ignore him. 'You, Sir Thomas ...?'

'I'd like a few minutes to rest, if I may, Inspector.' The old man's mouth was set in a thin, grim line. 'Could you perhaps deal with my guests first, so that some of the essential household work can be carried out? We shall be very short-handed as no one can get here from the village.'

'Very good, Sir Thomas.' After all, what difference did it make? 'Miss Clare?'

'Me?' She bounced up, and together they walked past the staircase through to the Incident room.

'I'm going to record this,' said Proby, as she made herself comfortable in the chair Rootham had brought in from outside. Oates had been sent to check on the state of the drive, and Allan was trying to get through on the car radio again.

'Goodness, you are clever.' She probably meant it. Tape recorders probably played as little part in her life as inter-stellar satellites. Or blunt instruments.

'May I have your full name, please, Miss Clare?'

'Dorothea Mary FitzGibbon Clare. There! It's quite a mouthful, isn't it? No wonder I've always been known as Dolly.' She beamed with delight.

'Born?'

'Inspector!'

'I have to ask.'

'The fifteenth of September, 1911. I weighed nine and a half pounds. And my wet-nurse was called Rosanagh O'Brien.' She was getting her own back.

'You live where?'

'Tommy lets me live rent-free in a very pretty house in the village. The Parsonage House. You must have come past it. It's got a thatched roof, blue shutters and a matching blue front door.'

'Tommy being Sir Thomas Hatton.'

'Yes. He's such a generous man. I've been a friend of Florence's for ever so many years.'

'Tell me about her.'

'Florence?' For the first time, the concept of her death, her *murder;* seemed to register with the little old lady. 'Oh dear.' She dabbed at her eyes, only succeeding in smudging the mascara. 'Poor Florence. I knew it would happen.'

Rootham, who had been almost dozing off in the corner sat up abruptly. 'You knew ...'

'Well, you see,' she looked at them both with an unexpectedly shrewd expression in her large vacant eyes, 'you're bound to find out. So there's no harm in telling, is there? She'd tried before.'

'Tried what?' Rootham stared at her.

'Why, to kill herself, of course. Several times that I know of. In fact,' she leant forward confidingly, 'she tried to pull me into the lake only a few days ago. "Come on, Dolly darling," she said ... she always called me that, "Dolly darling", in her lovely drawl. "Let's end it all together. It looks so peaceful down there among all those water-lilies." And the strange thing was, and this was what struck me most at the time,' she looked round at them both, and then lowered her voice dramatically, '*there wasn't a water-lily in sight.*'

Rootham stared harder, while Proby turned away to hide a smile. 'I'm sorry to have to tell you this,' he said after a moment, 'but Lady Hatton was murdered.'

Miss Clare's face hardened. 'Don't be ridiculous. my dear man. No one could possibly murder Florence. She was the dearest, kindest person ... she ...' Her voice died away. She shook her head slowly, twice, and then began to cry. Not softly, but in great tearing hiccups of grief.

'We'll talk again later,' said Proby kindly, rising, and helping her up by her elbow. Oates put his head cautiously round the door 'Take Miss Clare back to her room,' said Proby, 'and ask ... um ... Colonel Fetherstonehaugh if he could join us.'

'*Suicide*?' said Rootham when the old lady had hobbled out, still sobbing. 'Living in a bloody great palace like this. Money, servants? *Come on*!'

Proby shrugged. 'I expect it'll come clear.' His own experience had not led him to believe that richer people were happier. Rather the reverse, since increased time for leisure was also increased time to brood. And yet, by his conjectural reconstruction, Lady Hatton had struggled mightily to stay alive. And, as she had told him herself, she thought as little of servants as she did of policemen and central heating!

'*Here comes Colonel Mustard*,' whispered Rootham.

'Am I in the right place?' The Colonel was looking more like a tortoise than ever, gingerly extending his wrinkled neck round the door, and blinking anxiously as if expecting a violent rebuff.

'Come in, sir. Would you like to sit here?'

'Thank you, my dear fellow. All right if I smoke?' How could Proby say no, when the poor man would probably crumble to dust without his prop?

'Can you give me any reason why anyone should wish to murder Lady Hatton?'

The old soldier frowned, and inhaled heavily. This time Proby had the impression he was playing for time instead of nicotine. They had already established that he was eighty-seven, a veteran of General Auchinleck's African campaign and of Kenya before that.

'Well,' he said at last, 'I suppose there's always the money.'

'Can you expand on that?'

'John Boyce could give you all the details, of course. But Florence was a very wealthy woman in her own right.'

'Really?'

'Yes, really.' He wasn't used to being doubted. That was clear enough. 'She was brought up in California, you know. Belmont. Socking great place north of San Francisco. Museum now of course. We went there once, um, late fifties, they were knocked out to meet her. Absolutely knocked out. I know she'll have left most of it to the family, as you'd expect. But I dare say she left me something, and Dolly, though we're both very comfortable. But there were other bequests, I believe. Money's always a bummer in these cases. Am I right?'

'Quite right, Colonel,' agreed Proby. 'I'd like to ask you about something Miss Clare said.'

'Well?' The shakes were back, in a bad way.

'She said that Lady Hatton had tried to commit suicide, several times.'

The old man shielded his eyes for a moment. 'She wasn't well,' he muttered. 'In the blood. Both her brothers killed themselves. Can you believe that? What's odder is this: Tommy's brother did the same thing. Extraordinary. Between them they had three brothers, and all three topped themselves. But Dolly was a wonderful friend to her. They came out together, in the thirties. Seems extraordinary now. Lost world.' He coughed painfully and lit another cigarette.

'It seems that Lady Hatton died some time after midnight. I'm asking everyone this –'

'What were my movements?' He was shaking worse than ever, showering ash everywhere. 'Sat up with Tommy drinking port till about twelve. He went off to do some work, as he always does. Never stops! A great man in his own way. I went to bed. Next thing I heard that bloody cook screaming.'

'Your room is ...?'

'Up the red stairs across the way, first set of rooms, I got the left-hand one, next to Dolly Clare.'

'Where did the others go after dinner?'

He screwed up his eyes. 'Florence wasn't well, so she had dinner in bed. That wasn't unusual. Dolly and Emily went up to sit with her. Boyce stayed for a bit and then said he was turning in.'

'John Hatton?'

The Colonel's lip curled. 'No idea.' It was obvious he didn't care much either. 'He and that Humphrey fellow slunk off as soon as dinner was over. I must tell you ...' he leant over, dropping ash on Proby's knee, 'Tommy and I call him "*The Abominable Humph*"! Good, eh?' He rocked with laughter ending in another paroxysm of coughing.

'Lady Hatton's body was found unclothed,' said Proby. 'Does that surprise you?'

'Have you seen her room?' snapped the Colonel, suddenly icy.

'Yes?'

'Well, then. She wasn't a well woman. When she was upset, sometimes she would throw off her clothes. Or have a go at the furniture.'

Proby and Rootham stared at each other 'And you, Colonel? You were a friend of hers?'

'Don't be a damned fool,' growled the Colonel. 'We were lovers. Have,' he paused, '*had* been for more than thirty years. Now if you don't want anything else from me,' he had suddenly consulted his watch, 'I must go and do my duty.'

'Your ...?'

'When you reach my age,' said the old man testily, 'it pays to keep regular.' They let him go.

Chapter 8

'I realize you have to ask these questions.' There was no doubt that John Zeberdee Boyce was distinctly uneasy now that they had him on his own.

As soon as he had entered the room, Proby knew, with the instinct that comes only from experience, that the man had something to hide. But what? Bloody murder or some trifling peccadillo? So often the hardest task, in any investigation, was unravelling the twisted threads of which lies were important, and which irrelevant.

'It *is* necessary,' agreed Proby, with his blandest expression.

'Lady Hatton was a very wealthy woman.'

'So you've said,' put in Rootham, with a less bland edge to his voice.

'The main terms of her Will are very simple,' said the embattled lawyer 'She left some free American securities to Emily, the London house, its contents and one third of the residue to her son John, and two thirds of the residue to her elder surviving son Frederick.'

Proby raised his eyebrows. 'There's an elder son?'

'There were *two* elder sons,' Boyce corrected him, intertwining his fingers and stretching them. 'But Thomas, the eldest, died in a car crash twenty years ago.'

'Was he married?' put in Rootham.

'No.'

'Can you give us a rough estimate of what is involved by value?'

The lawyer shook his head. 'Impossible.'

'Half a million?'

Boyce laughed out loud. 'My dear Inspector! The American securities alone were worth over two million.' Rootham whistled.

'And the smaller bequests, then?'

Boyce screwed up his eyes and thought. 'It's difficult without the actual document ...'

'Which is where?'

'In a fireproof safe in my office.'

'That's your office in Castlewick?'

The lawyer inclined his gleaming head. 'Off the cuff, I'd say she left a hundred thousand to "Feathers", Colonel Fetherstonehaugh that is, and the same to Dolly Clare. Probably ten thousand or so to Miss Weissweiller and Maurice.' His eyes swivelled painfully away. 'A very generous lady.' And to the Colonel, thought Proby, though he kept his eyes, expressionless, on the face of the lawyer. He was beginning to sweat, just below the hairline.

'There will be a massive tax bill?'

'Indeed.' The lawyer paused, and then added, 'A number of the bequests were made free of tax.'

'Nothing to Sir Thomas?'

Boyce shook his head. 'At their age, that would hardly be sensible. Sir Thomas is, of course, a very wealthy man in his own right.'

'He owns the estate?' There was a very distinct pause. 'Please answer the question, Mr Boyce.'

Boyce licked his lips. At last he said, 'Not exactly.'

Proby leant forward. 'Tell me,' he said, 'who *exactly* does own it then? Land, house, and contents. In that order.'

Boyce stared at him. Then he said, 'Lady Hatton did.'

It was Proby's turn to stare. 'Lady Hatton? She owned everything?'

The lawyer nodded. 'Everything. Except some outlying farms that had been made over to Frederick, that's the elder son. He has about three thousand acres south of the river.'

And Lady Hatton?'

'The rest.'

'Extending to?'

Boyce shrugged. 'About twelve thousand acres. It used to be much more, of course. In the eighteenth century –'

'We only need deal with the position today,' cut in Proby impatiently. 'I'm still lost. How did Lady Hatton, from California, come to own Hatton Abbey?'

'Sir Thomas's father, the eighth baronet,' said Boyce, casting a sudden anxious glance over his shoulder, 'was very imprudent. Very imprudent indeed.'

'You mean he spent it all?'

'Worse than that!' said Boyce, warming to his subject. 'He'd managed to break the Trust latterly thanks to some new legislation. There were terrible debts. The whole place had to be sold.'

'But Sir Thomas had married a rich wife.'

'Well, not *exactly*,' said Boyce again, with a smirk. 'We're talking about nineteen thirty-five, remember. But there were family connections with California. And as the sale was being prepared, he went out there to plan a new life.'

'And came back with Miss Money-Bags!' said Rootham with a chuckle. 'Smooth operator.'

'It wasn't like that at all,' said Boyce, with an austere sniff. 'Lady Hatton's father, Senator Preston bought up all the debts and presented them to his daughter as a dowry. It all happened very discreetly.' He sounded most affronted.

'But you said Sir Thomas was rich in his own right?' persisted Proby.

'He has worked very hard, without let-up, for over fifty years. The holding company, which I administer, is all his own property, other than those shares that he has passed on to Frederick. There's the brewery, most of Castlewick New Town this side of the river, the Hatton shopping mall, and now he's building a new shopping centre in Hampton.'

'That big site in the High Street?' asked Rootham, suddenly impressed.

'Not bad for a man well over eighty.' Boyce smiled. He was obviously proud of his employer. And afraid of him too.

'So where were you after dinner last night?' said Proby.

'Me?' The lawyer's eyes bulged. 'I went to bed. I had a lot of work to do.'

'I gather you had the room next to Captain Humphrey's?'

'That's right.'

'What time did you hear him come to bed?' The sweating was worse now, a little rivulet had run right down his cheek and settled on his chin.

'I didn't,' he said. 'I must have dropped off to sleep. I don't remember anything.'

'Until the screaming?'

'What screaming?' he asked, startled.

'Mrs Freeman. When she found the body.'

'Good heavens!' laughed the lawyer, relieved. 'I couldn't possibly have heard any of that. I'm the other end of the gallery. No, what woke me was one of your men hammering on the front door. Just below my window. Never heard such a racket!'

'Thank you, Mr Boyce. I should like to see John Hatton if you can find him.'

'I'll go and get him,' said the lawyer, lumbering to his feet. He must have been six foot four at least, but obedience was second nature to him, at least when he was inside Hatton Abbey.

Chapter 9

In fact there was an involuntary pause in their investigations, as the butler appeared with the news that a breakfast table had been set up for them in the old Schoolroom, at the foot of the Back stairs in the basement, next to the kitchen, with breakfast now being served.

'Sir Thomas thought you would rather eat somewhere where you would be alone together. Of course, if you'd rather join him upstairs in the Dining Room …' His eyes, as ever, avoided Proby, focusing on some distant point. 'There is some water in the cellars below, but the basement is still dry. At the moment.' He compressed his ruby lips. He was obviously disturbed by the encroaching waters, but also, like Proby himself, enthralled by the perpetual drama of Nature unconfined.

'The old Schoolroom will be fine,' said Proby. 'I'll go and find the others.'

'They are already downstairs,' intoned the butler. 'They have locked both doors and taken both sets of keys. No one can get out.' He looked vaguely satisfied by this. No doubt it made his job that much easier. 'No one at all.'

'Thank you, Maurice,' said Proby gravely, earning himself a satirical look from Rootham. 'We'll be down shortly.'

After a bracing breakfast of fried eggs, bacon, sausages and black pudding, which Proby, Oates and Allan attacked with enthusiasm, they turned their attention to the police radio sets. Oates was, in his own way, quite an accomplished electrician, having completed an apprenticeship before deciding on the police as a career. For half an hour he tinkered with the gadgets, while Proby watched him impassively and Rootham occasionally tried to help.

'Im-possible,' said Oates at last.

'I told you that before,' said Allan, rubbing his eyes. 'I can't believe this. Trapped in this madhouse with a killer and we can't even call up the cavalry.'

Proby chuckled. It certainly was an unusual household. For most of them, death must have been a constant threat, for no other reason than the natural action of old age. Yet when one of them had at last died, it had taken a murderer to accomplish it.

His own main concern was for his wife, Sheila, waking in their cold silent house without even a message from him to say where or why he had left her so abruptly. That was not in itself unusual, but he wasn't happy about it, especially when she was not well.

'The helicopter pilot has a radio,' he said. 'We'll call the lads in when he gets back.'

'*If*, you mean,' said Rootham gloomily. 'If there's really been serious trouble at Rufus Down, they won't have time to worry about us here. They probably think we're having a smashing weekend with the country-house set.'

'You're not serious?' Allan couldn't stop thinking about his wife and baby. Or about whoever smashed the poor old woman's head in.

They were still speculating about the helicopter's return when John Hatton popped his head round the door.

'You all seem very much at home here,' he said. 'I must say, as a room, it's a very suitable choice.' It was an odd voice, high-pitched with just enough of a lisp to make it sound sneering.

'In that?'

'This is the Justice Room, Inspector. So-called because

in the old days this house functioned as the local magistrates' court.'

'It hardly seems big enough,' said Proby.

'There weren't many cases,' said the other 'When the sentence was death or transportation, you didn't get many people appearing twice.' He blew through his nose, a sort of liquid snort which evidently did service as a laugh.

'I'm very sorry about your mother,' said Proby, watching him carefully.

Hatton nodded. 'Thank you,' he said. 'But as I believe Feathers has told you, her hold on life was pretty involuntary. She didn't want to live, and we have all had to cope with the constant expectation that she would go. At any time.' He pulled out his cigarette holder. It was made of palest ivory, and intricately carved. 'Have you any idea how difficult that is?'

Proby shook his head. 'No,' he replied, 'but I can understand what you mean.' Even though that wasn't how Lady Hatton had appeared to him.

'The first time, you're aghast. How can you help her? What can be done? And the second time. And the third. By the time you get to the tenth, you're beginning to tire, to speak absolutely frankly.'

'This was murder.'

Hatton screwed in a thin black cigarette and lit it with a gold lighter 'Incredible,' he said. 'My mother was absolutely harmless. It makes no sense.'

'Money?' murmured Proby.

'*Money*?' Another snort. 'I don't know the exact terms of her Will, but none of us is short. I can't see anyone round her being that desperate.'

'Your own finances?'

He took it very well. 'Middling,' he said. 'My income is fifty thousand clear. I spend about sixty so I do have an overdraft, but it's not serious. Younger sons do have these problems, you know! When I get short, I come back to base for a bit. Less temptation, if you know what I mean?'

'To be specific?'

'Less dolly birds!' He winked at Rootham, who dropped his eyes, embarrassed.

'There is some suggestion that Colonel Fetherstonehaugh and your mother were ...?'

'Lovers? Some *suggestion*?' This time he hooted out loud. 'They've been going at it hammer and tongs since I first went to boarding school. I will say one thing for my mother. Whatever she enjoyed, she enjoyed in spades. Until she got ill ...' His voice tailed away.

'Your father didn't mind?'

Hatton shrugged. 'He's always had someone around.'

'Mrs Roberts?'

'I can see *you're* a detective. It certainly isn't Miss Weissweiller or Nanny Fisk!'

'Is that a long-standing arrangement?'

'Violet? More than thirty years, depending on whether you think she ever stopped fucking him for the brief moment she went off and married Frankie.'

'Do you like her?'

'Not much, but she's a good influence on my father, so that's in her favour.'

'Might they marry?' Softly put.

Hatton opened his mouth. 'That *is* an idea,' he said. 'Why not indeed? She'd like it. Though I don't think she was ever actually divorced from old Frankie. But if I were you,' he added thoughtfully, 'I wouldn't raise the question with my *father*. I think he'd consider it in very poor taste. Coming quite so soon after my mother's death, I mean.'

'I understand,' said Proby, watching him carefully. 'Now, about your own movements?'

'My movements?' He raised his eyebrows very high. It was a strange face, mobile, angular, with every sign of extreme, even finickety, care. Proby could almost believe that the eyebrows had been plucked, so delicately did they lie above his father's hooded eyes. For there was no doubt that he was his father's son, instead of, for example, the son of 'Feathers'. But where his father's face held a Roman stoicism, with all the stern implacablity of the archetypal graven image, this younger version with curving lips and large moist eyes, advertised a gimcrack strength, more likely to be implacable in seeking pleasure than in imposing self-discipline.

'Please.' Their eyes met and locked.

'Well ...' he said, slightly unnerved, so it seemed, for all the calculated hauteur. 'We all had dinner together. I'm sure you've gathered that already.' Proby said nothing. 'I don't share my father's or my brother's taste for long reveries over the port decanter, so Humph and I went off to play picquet in the Morning Room.'

'Why?'

'Why?' He was startled by the question. 'Because it's got a fire going all day.'

'The Morning Room is directly below your mother's bedroom?'

Hatton nodded. 'I'm very impressed. Some people take years to understand the geography here.'

'It's my job,' said Proby simply. 'Did you hear any movements overhead?'

'No,' was the reply. 'But I wouldn't have. The ceilings are too high in this house. And too well built. My ancestors built to last.' There was a sound from Rootham, indecipherable but probably unfriendly. 'In any case I went to bed early.'

'What time?'

'Elevenish. I can't swear exactly.'

'Captain Humphrey?'

'Went up the same time.'

'Your room is where?'

'Inspector! I'm disappointed. I was expecting you to tell me precisely where it was.' He was feeling more confident again. 'My room is at the top of the blue staircase, looking out over the forecourt.'

'And Captain Humphrey's?'

He shrugged. 'I can't remember, but I expect he's in one of the new rooms over the Dining Room.'

'Near your father's room?'

'There you are! You do know it all.'

'Tell me who's sleeping on the red staircase?'

'Feathers and Dolly Clare I think.'

'That is the staircase that goes on up to the rear of your mother's room, isn't it? I couldn't quite make out the Colonel's directions.'

'I expect he's on the lower mezzanine floor But you're quite right. If he went up another flight, that would take him to the rear of her room, past Mrs Freeman's room and the other room. Where my mother's nurse normally sleeps, but she couldn't get back this weekend.'

'And above her?'

'Up the very top, you mean? That's where Maurice and Edward have their rooms. Can you imagine? I've lived in this house for forty-seven years, and I've never been up to those rooms. Absurd!' He pulled what was clearly intended to be a comical face and tittered.

'As a child, you slept where?'

'Exactly where I am now. Up the blue staircase. Frederick and my late lamented eldest brother had the intermediate rooms, Nanny Fisk and a nurserymaid slept on the main floor, and Emily and I were tidied away at the very top. God knows what would have happened if there'd been a fire!'

'Can you think of any reason why one of the present household should have murdered your mother?'

He shook his head. 'It's unthinkable,' he said. 'It must have been an intruder.'

The next man in was Captain Humphrey, and it was immediately obvious that he had been drinking. His face was puce and his eyes were swimming and bloodshot.

'Hail, Inspector!'

'Please sit down, Captain Humphrey.'

'What if I'd rather stand?'

'At this stage,' said Proby, with a sinister smile, 'you may please yourself. But this may take some time.'

'You didn't have Johnnie for very long!'

'Perhaps we had less inquiries for him.' Again the sinister smile.

The Captain sat down. 'Just kidding!' He wheezed out something of a chuckle. 'Always one for a laugh.' He glanced at Rootham, who gave him a fixed immobile stare.

'First your details. Your full name, please.'

'Rupert Humphrey.'

'Date of birth?'

'Fourteenth, um, July, nineteen fifty-three.'

'Where?'

'Where?'

'Please.'

He frowned. 'Quettar.'

'Was your father in the army?'

'No,' he said shortly. 'Indian civil service. And damn badly treated by Mountbatten, I can tell you.'

'Your present address?'

'Well, that's a bit tricky. You see I've been lodging at the Coomber Club in Ealing. But we've had a bit of a tiff, so I'm putting up with Johnnie until I can get myself sorted out.'

'Do you have a job?'

He laughed, showing a lot of yellowed teeth. 'Not just at the moment.'

'Private income?'

'That's none of your damned business.' He was suddenly angry. 'What right have you got, prying into my affairs like this?'

'Would you like a solicitor present?' enquired Proby.

'Well, he'd have to be an Olympic swimmer, wouldn't he?' said the Captain, and laughed loudly. 'That's rather good. An Olympic *swimmer*!'

'Mr Boyce might be able to assist.'

'That pompous old creep! He can stuff it for a start!'

'May we return to your private income. I have to ask, because I need to assess your possible motives.'

'Motive?' shouted the Captain. 'Motive for what?'

'Lady Hatton has been murdered,' put in Rootham nastily. 'It can only be by one of the people present in the house. You are, of course, a suspect.'

'Oh?' He thought about this for a bit. '*Oh*?' He rubbed the back of his head. 'Well, I don't have much of a private income at all.'

'Does that mean none at all?' asked Rootham, his biro poised.

'Not everyone has their own private Trust invested by Cazenoves.'

'Like John Hatton, you mean?'

'He's a very generous friend.'

'He supports you?'

Silence.

'He supports you?'

'I don't suppose you've got a drink in here? I find I have to run on a pretty rich mixture away from town.'

'I'm afraid not.' Proby managed to sound genuinely regretful. 'John Hatton supports you?'

'He does. Sometimes. Sometimes I support him.'

'When was the last time you supported him?'

A crafty look came into the Captain's bloodshot eye. 'I think you should ask him about that.'

'So tell me about your movements last night.'

'After dinner, you mean?' Proby nodded. 'The old codgers were in full flow, droning on about the Dow Jones and all that. Johnnie and I sloped off to the Morning Room, he got Jeeves to make up the fire, and we settled down to picquet.'

'Why the fire?'

'Because it was damned cold, that's why. He got bored because I won, like I always do. So we went off to bed.'

'Together?'

This time the Captain really laughed. 'A couple of pooftahs, you mean?' He absolutely roared. 'No! Johnnie went off to his room, and I went to mine. Next to John Boyce.'

'This was ...?'

'God knows! Eleven? Thereabouts.'

'Did you go to sleep immediately?'

'More or less. Next thing I heard, that ghastly cook woman was screeching the house down. Right in my left earhole!'

Chapter 10

They broke for lunch, poached eggs on spinach, roast leg of lamb with vegetables and onion sauce, and finally a thick chocolate mousse with whipped cream. And as he ate the food, served by Edward, Proby's thoughts were on the poor twisted body upstairs in the sealed room. It was her money which had maintained the myth. And now she was dead, her skull smashed as she fled naked from her attacker, someone she could not help but recognize. Family? Friend? Servant? Husband, even? It turned the food sour in his mouth, and in the end he got up from the table while the others were still eating, and went over to the window to look out.

Even in this he was frustrated, for the glass was opaque, and shadowed by the thick grilles inside and out. The lower orders were clearly not intended to be distracted from their work by views of the garden.

'Back to work?' Rootham was draining a tiny cup of exquisite coffee. 'This is the life!' Edward was moving discreetly behind him, clearing away plates.

'Why are you avoiding me?' It was Emily Hatton. Standing in the doorway, she didn't even come up to his shoulders.

'I beg your pardon?'

'I want to talk to you. Can we go somewhere private?'

'Ahm-m.' It was Nero, expressionless as ever.

'Yes, Maurice?' She was breathing heavily.

'Daddy would like to speak to you.'

Daddy! It was all Proby could do not to laugh out loud. That terrifying old man! Soon he was going to have to question him too. She had quietly hurried away, leaving Proby with the butler.

'I'll have to ask you a few questions sometime this afternoon, Maurice.'

'When you're free, sir.'

Proby grinned, but the answering look was bleak and empty. An arctic cold. 'I'm free now, then,' he snapped, suddenly annoyed. 'Follow me, please,' and marched briskly back to the Justice Room, followed at a distance by his silent companion.

They found Rootham back in place, fitting a new tape. 'All well?'

'Yes, sir.' When had Rootham last called him sir?

'Take us through yesterday evening from the end of dinner. After you'd left Sir Thomas with the decanter, what then?'

'Mr John rang and wanted the fire made up there.'

'Was that usual?'

'It was Mrs Stinson's job. But her cottage is completely cut off. She hasn't been in since Wednesday evening. I told Edward to fetch over some more logs. If Chippington can't get across tomorrow, we're in danger of running out completely.'

'What fires are kept in all day?'

'The Drawing Room, the Library and Sir Thomas's bedroom are always lit first thing. It's not unusual for Lady Hatton to have a fire in the Morning Room if she's up.'

'And if she stays in bed?' Rootham at his most feline.

'Then there wouldn't normally be a need for a fire there.'

'You've told us you started here in nineteen forty-nine.' Had he? Proby simply hadn't noticed.

'It was very different then, of course. There were five men in the pantry under Mr Burton and a night watchman as well. Edward and I have to do all that they did, and more besides. I've told Sir Thomas ever so many times, but there's no telling some people.' As a piece of truth from the heart, this ranked as quite an unbending on the butler's part. He was beginning to sound almost normal.

'I gather it was Lady Hatton's money kept the place going?'

'I really couldn't say, sir.'

'Can you think of any reason why anyone should kill her?'

Maurice looked from one to the other, his eyes black pools of inscrutable emptiness. At length, after some subterranean effort, he said, 'She could be quite difficult sometimes. She didn't like Captain Humphrey.'

'Does anyone like Captain Humphrey?' said Proby humorously.

The black eyes reflected tiny flecks of light from the chandelier above their heads. 'He isn't very popular downstairs,' was all he would say.

As he was about to leave, Proby said, 'Were you asleep when you heard my men knocking on the doors?'

He shook his head. 'I'd heard Mrs Freeman screaming. So I started to get dressed. Then I heard the knocking a few minutes later.' Either it was true, or he'd seen the question coming. He had, after all, had all day to think of the answer as to why he was fully dressed in a tail coat at four o'clock in the morning.

Edward was a very different proposition. No sooner had he entered the room than he'd sat himself down, and lit a cigarette. 'Hands up who's recognized me.' The two policemen stared at him. 'There's a prize ...!'

'Why don't you just tell us?' growled Rootham, angry with himself for not having made the connection.

'Congratulations, boys. This is the big one!' Freed from his persona as servant, he was becoming quite a card. His was a chiselled face, neat and fresh, though the eyes, set rather too close together on either side of the sharp little nose, held a calculating expression.

'Let me think,' said Rootham. 'Great Train Robbery? The Gardner Museum Vermeer? Or Noddy's hooter?'

'Ha, ha.' Another man whose laugh lacked any sign of humour. 'Very droll.'

'Come on, Edward. Put us out of our misery.'

'I'm very disappointed, boys. I expected more from you, I really did. Remember the Buchanan diamonds? The Chatsworth snuff boxes?'

'*Geoffrey Parsons*? I thought they'd bagged you and thrown away the key!'

'*Arbeit macht frei.* I turned into teacher's pet. Lord Longford, Esther Rantzen ... you name them, I've laughed at their jokes. Now I'm going straight. Do you blame me?'

'In this house!' Rootham was staring at him, open-mouthed.

'Don't you want to know why I'm here?'

'Go on, then,' sighed Proby. 'Why are you here? As if we didn't know.'

'My old mum was born here. Sir Thomas gave me another chance. There's a decent man inside that gruff exterior, believe me.'

'How long has it lasted so far?'

'Just over eighteen months.'

'What can you tell us about the household?'

'Lots. I guess you picked up on Lady Hatton and the Colonel? And Sir Thomas and Mrs R.?' They nodded. 'Who says love ends at eighty? What about "The Abominable Humph"? He's got something on Master Johnnie. I don't know what it is but it must be serious because he has *carte blanche.* And then my lord and master, the silent Maurice. There's a man of few words. They called Lady Hatton mad, but Maurice has to go into St Michael's once a month for a check-up. And every now and then he books himself in for a week or so. You want to watch him. Especially when he's chopping up the firewood.'

'Mr Boyce?'

'A right villain. Creaming it off in half a dozen ways. He had a row with Sir Thomas fifteen, no, sixteen years ago. Wasn't much. They were driving back from Aintree in the big Daimler and Boycie contradicted something Sir Thomas wanted done. He stopped the car. Turfed him right out there and then. Onto an empty road at three in the morning! Pouring rain. And, what was worse, all in front of John and Emily. Any normal man'd have walked out. Not Boycie! He slunk back two days later, all smiles. But ever since, he's not missed a chance to skim off his share of the cream. I reckon he feels he's owed.'

'You're a goldmine, Edward.'

'Thank you, sir. And I'll tell you something about Miss Emily, just for free!'

'Go on,' said Proby, through frozen lips.

'She's straight as you'd find. A fine young lady. The man who gets her is lucky. Cheerio!' He just walked out before either of them thought to ask the questions about his movements the night before.

Chapter 11

Oates and Allan had dealt with the other servants, and had nothing unexpected to report from Miss Weiss-weiller or Mrs Freeman. The latter had volunteered to keep an eye on Lady Hatton when her nurse couldn't get back because of the floods. This had entailed peeping in to see her every three hours. She'd been tucked up in her pyjamas and sleeping the sleep of Temazepam at a quarter past midnight. At a quarter past three, she was still warm, but very dead.

'That leaves Sir Thomas, Mrs Roberts, Emily Hatton and, last but not least, Nanny Fisk,' said Rootham glumly.

'You and Oates see what you can get out of the formidable Miss Fisk,' said Proby. 'I'll go and see Sir Thomas and then Mrs Roberts in the Library. So far she seems to have the best potential motive, wouldn't you agree? Allan can come with me and take notes. Then I'll see Miss Hatton. That okay by you? And keep an eye open for that helicopter!'

Rootham shrugged. 'You're the gaffer.' There'd never been a sour word between them before that afternoon.

There was something about this house that was affecting them all. Despite the vast echoing spaces, there was a pronounced feeling of claustrophobia. And something else too. Proby looked around at his sullen subordinates. *Menace.* That was the other emotion the house inspired. For all its spaciousness, the fact that a killer was there with them, whether hidden or one of the outwardly harmless people they had met, lent an eerie *frisson* to every dark corner, every disembodied footstep. Twice Proby had caught himself gasping at a sudden sound – in full daylight!

He found, as he had expected, Sir Thomas in the Library

with Mrs Roberts beside him. She was reading a book aloud, but put it down as Proby entered.

'My turn?' enquired Sir Thomas politely. 'Perhaps you should leave us, my dear.'

She rose lightly and walked past Proby, flashing him a charming smile as she passed. 'I shall be in the Morning Room when you want me.'

'I've brought Detective Constable Allan with me to take notes, Sir Thomas.'

The old man nodded. 'As you choose.' He seemed to have lost much of his animation with the exit of Mrs Roberts.

'First, I'd like to repeat how very sorry I am about your wife.'

The old man's eyes flickered briefly over Proby's face. They seemed to approve. 'Thank you, Inspector.'

'Your own room is opposite Lady Hatton's, I believe.'

'Yes. That is so.'

'There is some reason to believe that Lady Hatton tried to fight off her murderer.' A spasm shook the heavy face. But no reply came. 'There must, I think, have been quite a lot of noise.'

Again the spasm. 'You're wondering how I came not to hear, and intervene?'

'Yes.' DC Allan was staring out of the window, appearing not to listen to their conversation.

'The reason is simple. I did not spend the night in my own room. Mrs Roberts has a room at the back of the house. Above us here, in fact. I joined her there.'

'I'm sorry to have to ask these questions, but they are essential if I am to apprehend the murderer.'

One hand was raised. 'I understand, Inspector. Perhaps it would help if I explained the situation. I loved, still love, my wife very much. But we have both, for many years, slept apart. I can't quite explain why this happened, my fault, I expect. But since we have always been the best of friends, we have tolerated each other's companions. Perhaps that has been made easier by our tastes being somewhat similar. I consider Alec Fetherstonehaugh as one of my oldest friends. I don't think my wife particularly liked Violet, Mrs Roberts that is, but they got on tolerably well.'

'It also avoided any difficulties over the estate, I imagine,' said Proby. It had to be said.

Sir Thomas's grim smile returned, momentarily, to acknowledge the hit. 'Very true,' he said. 'I see that you are well briefed. However, I really don't think either Florence or I considered that germane. And whatever others may think, it was our decisions that counted.' He nodded again, as if to reinforce the point. 'It was what first attracted me to her. That she shared my complete disinterest in the judgement of outsiders. An unusual thing in a young girl of twenty-three.'

'Can you suggest why someone in this house would have murdered her?'

Sir Thomas turned his head to look hard at the Inspector. 'Is it really as clear-cut as that?' he growled. 'Yes, I suppose it must be.' He sighed, an unexpected sound coming from so self-possessed a man.

'I understand that Maurice has intermittent psychological problems.'

'I'd as soon believe it of Miss Fisk as of Maurice,' said the other firmly. 'Yes, he gets a bit depressed. No, he has never shown any sign of violence. I've known Maurice since he was a child, playing in the stables here. There is no question of that. Not at all.'

'Edward?'

The baronet raised his eyebrows. 'Edward? Most convenient. You know, I am sure, of his past. I imagine he would take the first opportunity to acquaint you with it, being the sensible chap that he is. No.' Again he shook his head, though perhaps with a slight reluctance. 'I don't think so.'

'So who?'

'Do you know?' said the old man. 'I'd as soon believe that it was I myself as believe it of anyone else here.'

'Captain Humphrey?'

'*Captain Humphrey*!' The old man actually laughed. 'Do you know, I'd quite forgotten him. My dear Inspector, you must arrest him at once. At once! I've seldom met a man more fitted as a scapegoat. He certainly wouldn't be missed.'

'But you don't think he did it?'

The old man shook his head. 'I'm afraid not. Though I should dearly like to be proved wrong.'

'There's some suggestion he might have some hold over your son John ...'

'Who said that? Edward? Or Emily, perhaps?' He considered for a moment. 'It's possible. Probable, even. But I certainly don't propose to speculate about it. At my age one has earned the right to wear partial blinkers, don't you agree, Inspector?'

'I'm not quite sure what your age is, Sir Thomas?'

'I'm eighty-three, fast approaching eighty-four,' said the old man, with a hint of smugness. 'Now, it's time for my afternoon nap. Do you know what the worst thing about these damn floods is?' Proby waited. 'No daily papers. I really miss my hour and a quarter with the *Daily Telegraph*. Perhaps you would interview Violet, Mrs Roberts that is, somewhere else. Ask her to come to me when she is free. I want to talk it over with her. *Captain Humphrey* indeed!' His eyes began, very slowly, to dim and close. Rising together, Proby and Allan tiptoed out.

They found Mrs Roberts curled up decoratively in a tapestried armchair in the Morning Room, a pleasant room with pink silk on the walls and hung two deep with large canvases of seventeenth-century birds. There were parrots with angry red beaks, and cockatoos with swirling white plumes, farmyard cockerels and terrace peacocks, all jumbled together among ruined balustrades and overgrown urns in the most delightful confusion.

'Two of you!' She made it sound like a genuine compliment. She put down her book. 'How may I help?'

'Can you tell us first of your movements after dinner?'

'Starting as you mean to go on, Inspector?' She laughed. 'We had a fairly gloomy dinner.'

'Really? Why?'

'If one of you shuts that door, I might feel a bit more confident that everything I say to you won't be repeated.' At a look from Proby, Allan slipped across and closed the door. As he did so, he heard another door close, somewhere near at hand.

'Well?'

She uncrossed her legs and shifted in the chair to make herself more comfortable. 'Nobody likes Captain Humphrey,' she said. 'Nor Mr Boyce. We'd been quite a jolly party before they arrived.'

'How do you get on with Sir Thomas's children?'

She pursed her lips. 'I presume you know the situation? Yes? Well, we all coped. Johnnie's a bit of a prick, to be absolutely frank, but then he always was, even as a little boy. Frederick and Emily are very nice. They're protective of their mother, quite rightly so, but after all, when all's said and done, I've been around since they were children!'

'Do you mind telling me how old you are?'

'Not if you keep it to yourselves. I'm forty-eight.' He stared. 'I'm going to treat that rather blatant expression as a compliment,' she said, with an edgy chuckle.

'When did you first meet Sir Thomas?'

She smiled reflectively. 'When I was ten,' she said. 'He could have had me then if he'd wanted. His magnetism then, as now, absolutely bowled me over. I haven't wavered from him since.'

'Yet you married?' he queried softly.

She shrugged. 'There was an awkward moment when Florence conceived Emily and was going through one of her heavy emotional phases. Tommy thought it would look better. Frank, that's my husband, had been prowling around me with his tongue hanging out and I decided to go along with it. I was just sixteen! It wasn't a success, though that was probably my fault. Frank really got a pretty raw deal.'

'Where is he now?'

'God! I've *no* idea. The last I heard he was selling life insurance in Miami Beach!'

'Are you divorced?'

She shook her head. 'Tommy pays him quite a generous allowance. He's old-fashioned that way.' Proby caught Allan's puzzled frown out of the corner of his eye. 'I also think Florence may have preferred it that way.'

'You were brought up where?'

'Here!' she said. 'I thought you realized that. I was brought up here. My father was a tenant farmer just the other side of the main road. What you see of me now is Tommy's creation. He dresses me, always has, and he's taught me everything I know. Without him, who knows? I expect I'd be running a tea shop somewhere pretty dull!' She stretched out her arms and legs, like a drowsy cat. It was hard to believe that this slim elegant woman, the apparent embodiment of Parisian *chic*, had been a farm girl like, say, Mrs Freeman. What a household!

'So who do you think murdered Lady Hatton?'

She arched her long neck and smoothed her hair back. 'A burglar?' she tried hopefully.

He shook his head. 'She recognized him, or her.'

'How on earth can you know that?' she asked sharply.

'Just a hunch.'

She sat back. 'Then it's a highly improbable one. Did you know she was nearly blind? She could barely read even with her magnifying glass.'

'What exactly was wrong with her?'

She cocked her head. 'I don't think anyone really knew. Severe melancholia, something like that, I should say. Some days she'd be fine. Just as funny as when I first knew her, full of good jokes. Other days she'd be next to certifiable, throwing off her clothes, smashing windows. Quite scary, actually. If I'd had to guess, I'd have said she did it herself. But I suppose that's quite impossible?'

'Quite impossible. So tell me what you did after this gloomy dinner.'

'Me? I sat in here and finished the crossword, then I went upstairs, had a bath and got ready for bed.'

'You sat in here with John Hatton and Captain Humphrey?'

She snorted with disgust. 'Certainly not.'

'They say they were playing picquet in here.'

'Were they?' She blushed with embarrassment. 'How silly of me. Then I must have sat in the Saloon.'

'Did you sleep alone?'

She lay back and shrieked with laughter. 'Of *course* not! Really, Inspector. I may just be a simple country girl *au fond*, but I'm lucky enough to enjoy my side of a very agreeable bargain. Tommy's energy is amazing. And I expect he might say the same for me. He damn well ought to!' Allan didn't know where to look.

Proby racked his mind for something non-contentious to ask her. 'Do you know the terms of Lady Hatton's Will?'

'I can tell you one thing. I shan't be in it!'

'So what would you expect?'

'I'm sure most of it will go to Frederick with maybe something for Emily and John, although she'd settled trust funds on them ages ago.'

'Nothing for Sir Thomas?'

'Of course not. Oh, and Feathers, of course. She must

have left him something. He's such a dear man. And Dolly. She was lucky in her friends.'

After they'd left her, Allan wiping his brow in genuine perplexity, they went back through the Library, now empty, and found Emily Hatton sitting by herself beside the fire in the Saloon, quietly embroidering a cushion.

'May we disturb you?' asked Proby gently.

She looked up with a fierce, almost defiant, look in her large pale eyes. 'Are you feeling *protective*?' she snapped. 'Did you apologize for disturbing my father, or Feathers?'

Proby motioned Allan to a table behind the big settee. 'I'm very sorry about your mother,' he said, without altering his voice. 'I only met her the once but I can understand why ...'

'You can understand.' She said it flatly and her whole body suddenly shuddered. Unexpectedly she gave a little smile, and then assumed a satirical expression of polite enquiry. 'Do tell me, Inspector. Do you always talk in cliches? I mean,' she added, seeing his puzzled look, 'do you have this special *fireside* manner for all bereaved women, or only for young ones?'

'I don't mean to patronize you,' he said. 'Actually, I want you to tell me your movements last night.' He was quickly getting tired of *her* manner. Again she took him by surprise, this time because her whole face changed colour as he watched, flooding scarlet and then changing again to a mottled pink as her eyes filled with tears which began, silently, to pour down her cheeks. Yet still she stared at him. He looked away, and added, 'We can do this later.'

She shook her head violently, and angrily wiped her eyes. 'She was just so kind,' she said. 'So kind and harmless. Why would anyone hurt her?'

He nodded. 'Most crime seems pretty incomprehensible. Especially violence.'

She flicked her eyes again, almost squinting with the effort to control herself. 'You've no idea what living here is like,' she muttered, in a low tone. 'It's like a fucking waxworks. Everyone's so *old.* There are times when I feel violent, times when I'd like to burn this *bloody* mausoleum and all the lot of them. Valhalla here we come. I'm YOUNG!' The word burst from her like the cry of an angry bird. 'I want to live.'

Allan was busy scribbling, and Proby was hard pressed not to glance at him, to see how he was taking this new angle on luxury. 'It's not easy to remember how that feels,' he said soothingly, 'when one gets older.'

'God! Listen to Methuselah! Don't you realize, you look young to me, compared to all this ...' Her gesture took in both the fine old room and its fine old contents. No doubt she also intended to include her father's family and friends.

'I'm flattered.'

'You should be. My mother liked you. I was watching when you went to meet her.'

'From the staircase?'

'Did you notice me?' Allan had put down his pen and was staring at Proby.

'Yes. Now back to last night. What did you do after dinner?'

'Dinner! Talk about the Last Supper. No one spoke at all. Dolly, Dolly Clare, my mother's friend, and I left as soon as we could. We went to my mother's room. I read her part of *Farthing Hall.* It's her favourite book. Then, when she started to doze I went down to the kitchen to make her a milky coffee, and Dolly read her some prayers.'

'Did she have a hot drink every night?'

'Yes. Usually the nurse made it, but she wasn't here. I never left it, so I know it wasn't drugged. Just hot milk, some Nescaff and a little drop of maple syrup. She drank it down immediately.'

'What then?'

Her face began to colour again. 'I never saw her again. I just kissed her goodnight, and we left her there, all alone, not able to see …' The tears were beginning to run again. 'I loved her so much.'

'She had tried to kill herself,' said Proby, bracing himself for some outburst which never came.

'I know,' said Emily, with simple acceptance, 'but that was because she loved us. She hated the way her mind was failing, and her funny fits. No one else minded, but she did. Both her brothers killed themselves, years ago, in America. There's a strong streak of depression in her family.'

'Has it affected any of you?' he asked quietly.

She paused. 'Certainly not me, or Johnnie except on the subject of bank managers. We've been lucky.'

'You have an elder brother, I believe.'

'Fred? He's in Scotland. He drinks a bit too much, but he certainly isn't depressive. My father's such a dynamo, I think his genes have cancelled hers out!'

'So who do you think did it?' he asked, more out of genuine curiosity than to provoke her.

'Who d-do I think?' She was suddenly stuttering with anger. 'Who do I think b-battered my mother's head in? I thought that was your job. Isn't that why you and all these other creeps are poking about in our affairs?' She burst out into loud sobs.

'I'm sorry,' said Proby, rising. She'd certainly inherited her mother's unpredictability. 'But I should still like an answer.'

'I expect Nanny Fisk did it. She's always been a raging socialist!' She turned scornfully back to her embroidery, and Proby, after looking down at her for some moments, turned and gestured to Allan to follow him out of the room.

'Let's recap,' said Proby after they had returned to the Justice Room and compared notes with Rootham and

Oates. 'So far there's no one who couldn't have done it. And no evidence to show who did.

The people best placed would have been the people on the red staircase. That's the two menservants, Miss Clare and the Colonel. They only had to nip up or down a few steps, run into her room and do it.'

'And Mrs Freeman,' murmured Oates. 'Yes. We mustn't forget her.'

'I think they're the least likely,' said Rootham.

'Why?'

'It's only a tiny staircase. And some of the steps creak like anything. If there was any noise, they'd have been bound to have woken the others and risked being caught trying to get back to their room ...'

'So? They could have gone out into the gallery and down the main stairs. Back to their room that way.'

'That's be very hard to explain if someone saw you.'

'No one did.'

'I think Sir Thomas has got to be the prime suspect. He only had to cross the gallery, what, twenty feet, and then straight back before anyone woke up.'

'He's got an alibi. Mrs Roberts spent the whole night with him.'

'They were in it together?' hazarded Allan, who had stayed silent until now.

'That's possible,' conceded Proby. 'I wonder why no one heard her screaming.'

'Perhaps', said Rootham, 'she never did. If the lights failed, and she could hardly see, she may not have known what was going on. She may have thought it was a terrible nightmare.'

Chapter 12

As what little daylight they'd had dwindled into twilight, and darkness reclaimed the house despite or perhaps all the more because of the guttering candles, so too the pervading sense of fear returned. There was even a *smell* of fear, combining dank sweat with the rich mould of old tapestries and half-burnt candle-grease.

'You got any darts?' Even Oates realized that this question, addressed to Maurice, was doomed to oblivion. The butler raised a single, incredulous, eyebrow and passed on, bearing a soda siphon towards the Saloon.

'He gives me the creeps,' muttered Allan, watching the man's silent figure receding into the gloom.

'The whole place gives me the creeps,' agreed Oates, wiping his mouth for the tenth time in as many minutes. 'Are you worried about Beryl?'

'What do *you* think?' Allan rolled his eyes. 'It's no joke, coping with a newborn babe all on your own.'

Oates shrugged. 'I wouldn't know! I just …' A sudden shouting brought both men to their feet. 'Where?'

'THERE!'

Above their heads, on the landing of the great stairs, they could see a silhouette, a man gesticulating.

'WHAT?'

'Why are there no bloody candles on these stairs?' It was only Captain Humphrey, limping down and making a lot of noise doing so. 'Only twisted my fucking ankle! Where's that loony Maurice?'

'Sir Thomas wishes dinner to be served at eight o'clock.' Maurice had rematerialized beside them. If he had heard the insult, he gave no sign, preserving his invariable frozen face. But Proby, watching from a far doorway, caught just a flicker of something unexpected in those black hooded eyes, not so much a movement as a contraction of the pupils.

'And for us?' he asked lightly, crossing the corridor.

'The Old Schoolroom, sir. As before.' Close to, Maurice was unchanged. If it was a part he was playing, it was moulded onto him and was now, perhaps always had been, inseparable and indistinguishable from whatever lay within.

More steps. It was becoming a regular marketplace at the foot of the stairs. 'Sir Thomas has asked me to make up beds for you all.' A glance at Miss Weissweiller's expression told of her outraged disapproval. 'The Inspector is to sleep in the Tapestry Room, and there are three other beds in the rooms behind.'

They were still at it, puzzling over motive and opportunity, and none the wiser, nearly two hours later.

'Why won't these damned contraptions work?' Between them, they'd been trying to make contact with Headquarters all day. It was no good. Either their radios were hopelessly adrift or, more probably, something had gone wrong in Hampton. Nor had the helicopter reappeared. Twice Rootham had walked down the drive in the twilight to survey the flooding which isolated them from the village, and twice he came back with a long face to report that, if anything, it was getting deeper.

'One of us could get through by swimming,' said Oates thoughtfully.

Proby shook his head. 'I need you all here. We don't want another incident. Tonight I want one man on the main stairs and another on the move. We'll take it in turns. The other two can put their feet up in the bedrooms, so long as they're ready to come running. We'll review the situation tomorrow when we've had a chance to cross-check these stories.' He glanced at his watch. 'Eight o'clock. You lot go and have dinner. I'll stay in the Hall until one of you comes to relieve me. Not that I imagine anyone's in any further danger with us here.'

Sitting there, half dreaming in the golden flickering light, his thoughts again strayed back to Sheila, her lonely awakening, her pains, her whole generous, impulsive and utterly unpredictable personality. What pain she had brought him! And what pleasure too. His lips curled at the memory. A flare of light cut through the gallery, startling him from his reverie. Then another and a rumbling of thunder, distant but threatening. So. Another storm, just to add to their predicament. At least they were safe enough in this great barracks. He had hardly registered the thought when a crashing behind him sent him jumping to his feet, his face paling with unaccustomed panic, as a rush of air blew out the candles, plunging the hallway into darkness. Turning and ducking, with one arm half raised against an expected blow, he grabbed his torch, wielding it like a truncheon. In its glare, he could see the nearest shutter clattering backwards and forwards and the floor glistening with the reflected glitter of thick shards of broken glass. Whatever had struck the french window had splintered some of the glazing bars. Indeed he could see the culprit, a heavy branch, thick and wet, its blackened bark deeply scored and broken.

'What's happened?' He swung his torch. It was Boyce, carrying a tall candlestick which dripped wax onto the marble floor. He was wearing a dinner jacket, looking rather impressive with starched shirt-front and a heavy gold chain in his low waistcoat.

'Go back to your dinner,' said Proby sourly. 'We'll get this cleaned up.' He could hear rather than see the other policemen, their faces strained, running up from the basement towards him.

'It would be best to leave it.' Maurice again, calm but firm. 'Edward!'

'Coming!' Both men carried brooms. How had they known what would be needed? Even Mrs Freeman was getting in on the act, carrying a dustpan and getting down on her knees amongst the broken glass. Sir Thomas, reflected Proby, watching and admiring the easy efficiency of a perfectly trained household, was very well served.

It was midnight, and the thunder had died away, before Mrs Roberts, her embroidery in one hand and her candle in the other, slipped out into the gallery and began to climb the stairs.

'Good night!' she called softly to the watching Oates, slumped uncomfortably in the leather armchair on the landing with an oil lamp beside him, a vantage point whence he could, more or less, observe both floors.

'Good night, miss.' He watched her figure, so slim and lithe, as she climbed away from him, and she added a little wiggle of her bottom with him in mind.

'That'll keep the poor boy awake!' she thought wickedly. She loved this staircase, the antithesis of everything she had known as a child in the dingy farmhouse with its low ceilings, damp walls, and just a single lavatory, at the bottom of the garden. And the price had been no more than to please the man she loved. Perhaps she should have left it there. She glanced back at the policeman. There was a risk, of course. But no risk, no reward, or so her father had taught her, in between molesting her. And the reward was to be very great indeed.

She slipped along the gallery, past the door to Lady Hatton's room, now secured with striped tape, and tiptoed into Sir Thomas's bedroom opposite, suppressing a little shiver as she did so.

'Hello, my dear!' He was propped up in bed, reading by the light of a dozen candles in a bronze candelabrum, but put down the book, a heavy ledger, on seeing her. She bounded onto the bed, a massive four-poster upholstered in crimson and black stamped velvet.

'Feeling playful?'

He shook his head. 'Not tonight.'

She pouted. 'I'm sure I could …'

'I've no doubt you could,' he said, running one hand lovingly over her body. 'But I must catch up on my homework.'

'At midnight!'

'Until it's finished,' he said.

'You love your work.'

He nodded. 'And I love you.'

She nestled against him. 'I'm so sorry about Florence.'

He looked down at her, so beautiful, and so spirited. How had he deserved the good fortune to attract this tigress who had, by chance, been born on his very doorstep? 'It's very puzzling.'

'Do you think they'll catch whoever did it?'

'Oh, yes,' he said. 'Proby's an excellent officer. He'll solve it.'

'There might be trouble between him and Emily.'

The wandering hand stopped. 'Really?'

'It's strange, isn't it? How people pair up.'

'No stranger than you and me. The age gap must be about the same.'

'You're different!'

'So are you.'

'Show me then!'

He chuckled. 'Very well!' and reached round to undress her.

An hour later she left him, snoring quietly, and slipped out through the passage at the back of his room. This led into a maze of small rooms overlooking the church to the west of the house. She hadn't bothered to put her clothes back on and just threw them in a heap beside the clothes basket. Then still naked, she stepped back into the corridor and walked down to her bathroom and turned on the taps. Five minutes later she was soaking herself luxuriously in the steaming water, made aromatic by a rich green preparation which she had added liberally from a glass decanter 'Who's that?' she called sharply, hearing a footstep. 'Oh, it's you.'

'I thought we ought to talk?

'Damn right. Pass me the soap.'

'Here you are. You're lucky to have kept your figure.'

She was soaping her breasts. 'I know. It is rather good, isn't it?'

'Do the police know anything?'

'How can they? I've done my part. Now it's your turn.'

'That's just how I see it.'

Two hands seized her round the neck and, before she could scream, plunged her head under the water. Her legs thrashed desperately, but the pressure of the fingers was too strong. That lovely body, designed for and dedicated to the pleasure of men, arched, shuddered and then fell slack, in a grotesque echo of her earlier love-making. After a few minutes, her visitor slipped quietly away, though not without blowing out her candle with a triumphant smile.

Chapter 13

With the dawn, a tentative yellowish dawn that crept across the sodden landscape, battered by the previous night's storm, like a bush fire before subsiding behind a renewed curtain of driving rain, it became apparent that the waters were still rising. For one thing there was a distinct smell of damp and decay in the basement. There were even puddles in the kitchen. And when Edward, returned in his dungarees from stoking the house boiler with damp anthracite from the heap behind the stable wall, mopped them up, they were back again by the time Mrs Freeman had finished frying the bacon for breakfast.

What was more, when Allan went out to check their car, he found it gone! For a dreadful moment he thought perhaps the murderer had made off in it. Just the thought of facing Proby with this news was enough to set the poor man shaking. But then he saw it – floating upside down a quarter of a mile away in amongst the tops of some young trees. What a mess! How could anyone maintain a marriage with this sort of thing going on? He trudged furiously back to the house.

Proby, in between his stretches of sentry duty, had slept fitfully but well in a huge old bed hung with faded tapestry. There were more tapestries round the walls, and indeed the whole room held a vague but pervasive scent of decayed canvas. He had left his curtains open, so was surprised, even dismayed, to wake and find it already past eight o'clock and full, if water-logged, daylight.

The bed was astonishingly soft, and it was years since he had enjoyed the authentic comfort of linen sheets. For a moment he sank back, indulging an older man's relish of rest, but then, brusquely remembering, he flung back the seductive weight of the bedclothes and made himself leave the bed. He padded across to the window, in time to see the disconsolate figure of Allan climbing the entrance stairway below. Entering the bathroom, he could hear Oates snoring in the low room next door.

A hurried shave, with one of the four razors thoughtfully supplied by, presumably, Miss Weissweiller, a general splash of water, luxuriously hot as soon as he turned the tap, and he was quickly dressed and on his way down the main stairs, feeling almost at home!

Rootham, who had taken Oates's place on the landing, stood up as he approached.

'All quiet?'

'One or two people about. Maurice took a tray up to Sir Thomas ten minutes ago, and Edward has been about since six, opening up and lighting the fires. The old dragon ...'

'Nanny Fisk?'

'Her! She's been mooching about, muttering under her breath.'

'Mrs Freeman?'

'Haven't seen her. But I smelt bacon a while ago, so I imagine she's down there somewhere. No one else, though. You going for breakfast?'

'Yes. Come on. You've done your bit here. Afterwards I'd like to go through the statements again. Something someone said surprised me. I just can't remember what it was.'

But no sooner had they sat down than Edward, white in the face, ran into the room.

'It's Mrs Roberts!'

'What?' Proby started up.

'She's in her bath. Drowned!' He slumped against the table, shaking. 'She's dead.'

Looking down on the corpse, on this soft and sculptured woman who was still as beautiful in death as she had been in life, Proby was suddenly assailed by the thought of his own death. How would that come about? What, when it came to that, would he most regret? To his surprise he found himself thinking of a tree, seen through a window. The tree filled the window and was dancing in the wind, each branch, each tendril, waving in counterpoint, oblivious of each other, as the gale shook and buffeted the pale and delicate leaves. Spring then, and not at his home in the Dales either, since it was a tall window, through which he watched, enthralled, the silent gaiety of the dancing tree.

'This is *wrong*.' Sir Thomas had entered without Proby knowing it, and was gazing down at the woman he had loved. There was, in his grim old eyes, an indescribable hurt, so much so that Proby turned away. At last the old man seemed to regather his self-control. He looked up at Proby and said, through gritted teeth, '*Evil*'. Then, turning abruptly on his heel, he walked out again, with slow steady tread.

'Time of death?' Even Rootham seemed moved. They'd decided to get her body out and had carried it dripping through to her bedroom. It was immediately apparent that she had been strangled.

'Impossible to say. For one thing we can't know what temperature the bath water was. Oates says she went upstairs at midnight and turned down towards Sir Thomas's room. He swears she didn't come back, so she must have gone out through his dressing room and round the back. We'll get a statement off him later. I think he should have an hour or so to himself.'

Rootham nodded. There was a humanity to Proby which he had always admired. Others might have gone straight for the old man while he was still in shock, hoping to force something out of him. But then others didn't have Proby's track record. He could, perhaps, afford to be generous.

Proby felt her arm. 'I'd say she'd been in the water several hours.'

'Who could have got to her?'

'Humphrey and Boyce are just down the same corridor And Sir Thomas. Anyone else would have had to come through our rooms, or cross the Hall in front of whoever was on the stairs.'

'Quite apart from dodging you and me?' While Oates and Allan had taken it in turns on the stairs, Proby and Rootham had divided the other watch, tramping softly round the old house.

Proby nodded. 'It was a mistake to use torches. Whoever it was could have seen us coming by the light.'

'He must have an iron nerve!'

'Unless it's Boyce or Humphrey.'

Rootham took another look at the bruising on her neck. 'Could a woman have done this?'

'I'd say so. She must have been taken by surprise. Wouldn't have had much chance, all slippery in the bath. In fact, I rather think ...' He paused, deep in thought. 'Whoever did it must have come round from the door ...'

'You mean ...?'

'She couldn't have been taken by surprise. Who would your Mollie be most likely to receive in her bath?'

'Another woman!'

'It's a thought.'

They looked at each other 'Mrs Freeman?' said Rootham. But they were both thinking the same thing: that made Emily, as the most active, so the most suspect.

Divided into the same two teams, they spent the next two hours interrogating everyone in the house except Sir Thomas. There were no surprises. Each person claimed to have gone to their room and stayed there all night. Boyce admitted using the bathroom he shared with Humphrey at about three in the morning.

But he asserted that he had neither seen nor heard anything.

'He's hiding something,' said Rootham, after the lawyer had left. 'No one sweats that much without a guilty reason.'

'I agree. We'll see him again after lunch. Now I'll go and talk to Sir Thomas alone.'

Proby left the Justice Room and, walking round under the great stairs, he turned left down towards the Library. Sure enough, Sir Thomas was standing in front of the fire, while Edward, on his knees, was trying to blow some life into the smouldering wood with a large pair of old bellows.

Dismissing him, the old man gestured to a chair for Proby before carefully closing the door into the Saloon. 'Thank you for allowing me time to recover,' he said. Proby, watching him covertly, was impressed by the man's resilience. The stern face was back under complete control, impassive and receptive at the same time. 'I want you to promise me one thing.' Proby waited, impassive. 'Whatever pressure is brought to bear on you, I want you to promise that you will solve this crime and bring the murderer to justice.'

'I can promise you that I shall do my best.'

'*Fiat justitia ruat coelum*,' said Sir Thomas. 'Which I will translate for you as "Let justice be done though the heavens fall." An excellent motto for those with nothing to fear,' he added drily. Then: 'Mrs Roberts was the best friend anybody could have hoped to have.'

It was Proby's turn to look away. 'It must have all happened very quickly,' he said.

'I pray so,' said the old man in a low voice. 'Extraordinary that she should have given so many years to me. I never doubted that she loved me.' His eyes swivelled inwards. 'Strange as it must seem.'

'*De gustibus non est disputandum*?' murmured Proby.

'Forgive me,' said the old man, looking up sharply. 'I had no idea that you were a Latin scholar else I should not have patronized you by translating the Gaius Frontinus.'

Proby grinned. 'A few tags picked up from a generous teacher do not amount to scholarship. But it impresses the Chief Constable.'

Sir Thomas actually smiled. 'I find it quite hard to imagine you and he working in harmony. You are married?' Proby nodded, unhappy at the direction of the conversation. 'For many years?'

'Nearly twenty.' A trifling exaggeration, well justified. It was extraordinary to think that he must seem almost a young man to this indomitable survivor.

'Hmm.' The old man blew his nose loudly and wiped his eyes. 'Now what can I tell you?'

'My officer says Mrs Roberts went to your room last night around midnight.'

'That is so. I was working on some accounts. She came to say goodnight.'

Proby stared at the flames licking round the logs. 'And stayed.'

'And stayed.' Although he was carefully not looking at the old man, he could identify the depth of grateful tenderness in the reply. 'It will be relevant, so I should tell you that we made love.'

'What time did she leave you?' asked Proby, turning his eyes to watch the other's reply.

He sighed. 'I don't know. I must have dropped off to sleep. Maurice called me with my breakfast as usual.'

'Were you surprised that she had gone.'

'Oh, no. It was quite unusual for her to stay the night. She did keep some clothes here, but I can't recall the last time she spent two consecutive nights under my roof. I assumed she'd gone off to her own bed, and that she would join me after breakfast.'

'I need to ask you again about Thursday night.'

'I see.' A dry response which sounded as if that did not come as a surprise. Sir Thomas was evidently a man who thought things through very carefully and very quickly.

'You told me yesterday that you and Mrs Roberts spent the whole night together.'

'I know.'

'Was that not true?'

The ironic smile was back. 'It was true. But it was, in my experience, unique. To wake and find her still beside me, in my own bed ...' A single tear welled in his eye, and then, very slowly, trickled down his cheek. He brushed it aside impatiently.

'She could not have been involved in your wife's death?'

The expression in Sir Thomas's eyes for once defied Proby's analysis. 'Not without involving me,' was the eventual reply in a steady voice. 'No.'

'I'm trying to make sense of her death,' said Proby, who was, to be truthful, floundering.

'It's as incomprehensible as Florence's,' said the old man, 'unless someone is trying to hurt me.'

'How often do you go to London?'

'Once a fortnight. Sometimes more often.'

'Will her leaving the London house to your son John make any difference?'

'I don't understand.'

'Well, will the fact that the London house which belonged to her now belongs to your son John affect your own arrangements?'

'You've discussed my wife's Will with Mr Boyce, I take it?'

'Yes. I needed to know the main provisions.'

'And he told you ... what?'

'That your elder son got two thirds of the residue,

Emily got roughly half a million pounds in US securities and John got the London house, its contents and one third of the residue.'

'Remarkable.'

'You weren't expecting anything to be left to you?'

'Indeed not. My wife and I had been long agreed that neither would add to the other's capacity for contributing to the present Government.' Yet something had upset him. Behind the impassive mask, something was wrong.

'You still can't think of any reason why either of these two ladies should be attacked.'

'No, Inspector. Now I should like to rest.' Proby nodded and made for the door 'Inspector!'

He turned. 'Yes, Sir Thomas?'

'Without electricity, the bells in this house no longer work. If you should see Maurice or Edward, would you say I'd be grateful for a word?'

'Very good, Sir Thomas.' He seemed to be slipping quite happily into the role of family retainer himself! Perhaps it was just a courteous way of speaking that made an order acceptable.

He discharged his errand by finding Edward coming out of his bedroom. 'Miss Weissweiller asked me to lay out some clothes for you,' he said, with an unprofessional wink, 'as you may be here for some time. She reckons you're the same size as Her Ladyship's godson, who left some things behind last week. There's a couple of dress shirts and a spare pair of jeans. If you want to try them on, Mrs Freeman will launder those for you.' He cast an expert eye over Proby's rumpled suit.

Uncertain whether to be grateful or offended Proby told him to go to Sir Thomas, and went into his room. The shirt and trousers fitted rather well.

'You look much nicer like that.'

Emily was standing in the doorway. Although her face was serious, there was a pleasant warmth in her gaze.

'Your father's very upset,' he said, conscious of a constriction in his throat. What was it about this woman? He knew that he loved Sheila, indeed was thinking about her constantly. Yet, here, in an alien setting, something inside him seemed able to cast loose, freeing him to run risks with his emotions in a way that he did not understand.

'Let me take these things down,' she said, coming over to the bed, and gathering up the dirty laundry.

'I'd better hang on to my wallet.'

She felt in the jacket pocket and passed it over to him. 'No gun?'

'Certainly not!'

'I wouldn't mind having one.'

'Are there any in the house?'

'I'm sure my father has one. There used to be a whole rack of shotguns in the Justice Room, but Prentice keeps them now.'

'Prentice?'

'The head keeper. He lives about three miles away, by Wickham Wood.'

'You never left your room last night?'

She put the clothes down and came close, looking up at him as he towered over her. 'No. Does that surprise you?'

He frowned. 'No.'

'I sleep up there, you know. Right over your bathroom.'

'Next to John?'

'Absolutely. Have done all my life.'

'You get on with him?'

'More or less.' She shrugged as she spoke.

'What about Captain Humphrey?'

'*Abominable*!' He chuckled. 'I wish you'd do that more often.'

'I don't understand.'

'You may understand criminals, who are mostly men. But it's very clear you don't understand women!' Proby closed his eyes. It was probably true. Certainly, he had never understood Sheila. 'Men just go their own way, doggedly getting on with the job, don't they?'

'I think,' said Proby, smiling, 'that you may be judging all men against your father.'

'And why not?' she retorted hotly. 'He is a fine man. And I love him. And revere him.'

'Aren't you frightened of him?'

She laughed. 'Only other men are frightened of him. No woman has ever had anything to fear from him.'

'How old was he when you were born?'

She frowned. 'My mother was forty-five, so he must have been forty-nine.'

So! thought Proby. You are thirty-two years old. And I am fifty-six! And I fancy you like mad.

'What are you thinking?'

'I was wondering how old your brother was,' said Proby desperately.

'No, you weren't,' she replied, still laughing. 'You want to screw, don't you? Well, why not? Come on! I'd like it.' She was tugging him towards the bed.

He himself had been twenty-four years old when she was born. If his then girl-friend, Ruth was it? had conceived, he might have a daughter this age. In which case might he have desired her? For that matter, did Sir Thomas ever ...?

He seized her hand, which was already at his waistband. 'Wait,' he said. 'You've given me an idea. Were you ever jealous of Mrs Roberts's relations with your father?'

She stopped, amazed. 'Of course not! Why should I have been? Oh!' Her face flushed crimson.

'You mean do I fancy old codgers, because I want to

fuck my father?' She stepped back from him. 'What a filthy thought. You're just a disgusting old man like the others.'

He wanted to ask her which others, but she had run out of the room.

Chapter 14

As he came down the main stairs, he met Boyce coming up. The man's face was white, and he brushed past the Inspector as if he wasn't there.

'One moment, Mr Boyce ...?'

The lawyer ignored him, and hurried out of sight. Shrugging, Proby continued downstairs.

Letting himself out of the front door with the second set of keys, which he had annexed for his own use, he strolled down the horseshoe stone staircase and walked halfway across the gravel courtyard before stopping and turning to look back at the house.

There was another lull in the rain, and for a while he stood enjoying the buffeting of the light westerly breeze against his face. It was good to breathe fresh air after the fumes of the methylated-spirit lamps in the corridors inside.

He stared up at the façade. The architect had pulled off quite a remarkable trick. Raised on the low, barred basement were the two rows of towering windows, apparently announcing two rows of towering rooms. There in the middle was the wider, arched window of this end of the gallery. To its left the two high windows of his own bedroom. But the remaining three windows served two floors, as did the three below them. That window there, for example. Its bottom half lit his bathroom, whereas its upper half lit Emily's bedroom, the room where she would receive him if ...

He rubbed his head to clear his thoughts. He stared at the window. Now that he knew what lay behind, he could see the thick line of the dividing floor.

Walking round to the east, a different approach had been adopted and each of the five floors, from basement to attic received their due acknowledgement, clustered round the truly titanic scale of the central window, forty feet high at least, which lit the great stairs.

From the inside it seemed to preside over the staircase with an almost mythic presence. Certainly one that defied rational analysis. From the outside however, he could make a more mundane judgement, that it was, regardless of any theatrical properties, a genuinely extraordinary feat of engineering! Water was everywhere. The ground must have dipped, disguised perhaps by a sleight-of-hand with the basement's dimensions, because on this side of the house little wavelets lapped at the walls themselves.

And then he thought about Sir Thomas, so small, so old, and yet so staunchly resilient in the face of personal tragedy. Proby himself, well over six foot, his substantial bulk freed from stolidity by his weekly sessions at the police gym, was so used to dominating or at least matching those about him, that he could only speculate about the burden faced by a young man, physically minimal, crushed by the improvidence of his father. Yet Sir Thomas had emerged doubly triumphant, with his heritage intact, to found a new race of semi-dwarfs to inhabit this exquisite building where he had spent the last forty years or so with his two women and his own burgeoning career.

So why, pondered Proby, looking up at the garden front which echoed that overlooking the forecourt, with its massive double row of high windows, would he go and murder them both on two consecutive nights? There was no question that he was the one person with the greatest opportunity. Yet he was also, it seemed, the man with the most to lose. Unless ...

Proby had been about to turn the corner, paddling through the shallows, in order to examine the fourth façade, but instead he turned and hurried up the garden steps, letting himself in through the second door, and sent Oates to find Colonel Fetherstonehaugh.

Another old man! Older even than his host, but with a similar record of unusual sexual fidelity unconsecrated by marriage.

'Please sit down, Colonel. Thank you for coming.'

'My dear fellow!' The Colonel seemed, if anything, a little less frail today, with his freckles retreating into the landscape of skin a healthier pink.

'I need to ask you more specifically about your relations with Lady Hatton.'

'Indeed?' Very frosty. He took out a gold cigarette case and lit up, this time without asking permission.

'You and she had been lovers for thirty or so years.'

'Correct.' His pale blue eyes met Proby's bland stare with a corrosive antagonism. No one, Proby reminded himself, reached the rank of Colonel through being an agreeable old buffer. That just came later, if it was the sort of part you were happy to play.

'Did you ever ask her to marry you?'

The Colonel coughed with contempt. 'No,' he said.

'Did …'

But the Colonel had stood up, shaking in his agitation. He wasn't finished with the last question. 'That is a ridiculous and *outrageous* suggestion. How could anyone think that I would threaten my darling Florence's happiness in such a *crass* way?' He was spitting the words out. There was more to come too. 'Of course I can see which way your *mind* is heading. You think Florence was planning to *leave* with me, so Tommy or John killed her to save this place.' Spot on. 'Do you *really* think either she or I would ruin a whole *lifetime's* commitment? She loved this place, and she loved Tommy, very much. She would never have *dreamt* of leaving, nor I of asking her to do so.' He subsided, wracked by a fit of coughing. When he had recovered, his face now scarlet, he lit another cigarette.

Proby watched him for a moment. 'If Lady Hatton was so happy and fulfilled,' he said remorselessly, 'why did she repeatedly try to kill herself?'

The old soldier shrugged. His calm was evidence that he had had to face up to the same inconsistency too long ago for him to take offence at the subject. 'She was ill. Genuinely ill, I mean. There is so much confusion about mental illnesses. Many people think of behaviour changes as voluntary, and of course in some people they are. Florence wasn't like that. When she was well, she was such a lovely person, so gay and full of fun. You must believe that, because most people remember only the bad times.' Proby nodded. He had only met Lady Hatton the once, but she had impressed him strongly as a good woman. 'And now that she's dead, that will be even more true,' said the old man sadly. He inhaled deeply. 'When Tommy and I are gone, her grandchildren will no doubt joke about their "mad" ancestor. They won't remember her as the most generous and *funny* person I ever had the privilege to meet. Did you know that she was a *brilliant* pianist?' He raised his head, his eyes distant now. 'I don't mean a gifted amateur. She was concert standard ... studied with Rubinstein ... she ...' His voice was beginning to trail away. 'I'll tell you something else,' he added, coming back to earth. 'For all that Tommy loved Violet, and by God she was a beautiful young woman, *shockingly* beautiful if you understand what I mean, and sexy as all hell ...' He had lost the thread of his thought. 'Oh, yes!' He smiled fondly. 'Well! He never, ever, made Florence wait for a single meal. In the days when he was always tom-catting off into Hampton to join Violet, he'd set her up in a very handsome old house near the Close, you probably know it, don't you come from Hampton? ...' Proby waited patiently. 'No? It's just behind the Diocesan Office? At the back there, somewhere.' Proby nodded to keep the old boy happy. 'There! I knew you'd know it.

Well, he was always back on time for meals. To show his respect. Not embarrassing her in front of the servants, you understand? Not that they didn't all know, because they'd all grown up with little Violet. I bet old Maurice fancied his chances!'

'Maurice the butler?' Proby was astounded. He'd taken the man to be entirely sexless.

'Oh my *God* yes!' The Colonel threw back his head and laughed. 'Maurice was quite a pasha with the estate girls. Florence caught him once hard at it with one of the maids, I can't remember which now, *under the kitchen table.* There was a right old hoo-ha about that, I can tell you. He was only a junior footman in those days. I mean, I'm going back forty years or more, before my time even.'

'I see. That is most interesting.'

After he'd hobbled out, Proby leant back in his chair. Three miles across the river, a busy city hummed with the innumerable daily problems of a hundred thousand people. Anniversaries, petty crimes, the daily successes and failures of family and working lives, lives that he had come, gradually, to understand. And it was because he understood that he was able to preside over the attempted maintenance of a legal framework for these lives, a constraint against the worst excesses of wrong-doing.

But these old people, in their hermetically sealed container, this old *house,* with its very architecture an exercise in grandiose deception, and all those who accepted the deceptions ... he did not understand, not at all. And now, here they were, all four of them, walled up alive in the very same container, trying to make sense of a double killing, and with the murderer still very much on the loose among them, preparing even now, perhaps, to strike again if necessary. The trouble was, he thought, darting an anxious look behind him, that he had not the first idea as to who was responsible.

Nor did he feel any further forward when, climbing the great stairs in search of Rootham, he heard the leaden tread of Sir Thomas, walking up and down, up and down, along the first-floor gallery.

'Inspector?' Advancing through the door, he met the old man on the turn, his head sunk heavily on his chest, as he repeated and repeated his dreary patrol.

'Yes, Sir Thomas?'

'Come, I want to show you something particular. This portrait here,' the one immediately facing the door to the stairs through which Proby had just come, 'is the first Sir Thomas, knighted by Charles I when he stayed here, in the earlier house, of course, the one down by the river.'

Proby looked up at the picture. A pale man, with lace at his throat. And nothing like his descendant. Should he admire the *paintwork* or something like that? 'He looks, well, rather ill ...' He was trying to say something positive.

The old man chuckled. 'Well he might. It was painted from his death mask. He was killed at the Battle of Newbury. Now come and look out here ...'

They walked, at Sir Thomas's slow pace, to the far end, where the whole wall was given over to glass. 'Look!'

Water! It was everywhere, even among the parterres now. Here and there the head of a statue stared reproachfully up from among the brackish flood. But they might have been at sea for all the dry land they could see.

Amazing,' said Proby. It was the best he could do. Suddenly instead of a doll's house, he felt as if they were all adrift in a tall carved galleon, at the mercy of malignant seas. A heavy wind was moaning through the cracks. He even seemed to feel the floor of the old house heave beneath him.

'The first Sir Thomas had great plans for damming the river,' went on his host. 'In some ways he was the first landscape gardener. Except that the Roundheads polished him off at the age of twenty-eight, before he could put it into practice. I was thinking just now how he would have appreciated this view.'

Proby stared out across the trackless waters. This man had lost his wife, struck down as she fled screaming from her killer. He had lost his mistress, strangled mercilessly in her bath. And all in little more than twenty-four hours. Yet he was principally occupied with admiring a new perspective to his property. 'Remarkable,' he said. And meant it.

Unexpectedly, Sir Thomas chuckled. 'You've found out my Achilles heel, haven't you?' he said, casting Proby a sideways glint of his grim old smile. 'Family piety. What those without pedigrees of their own call snobbery. Well, well, I admit it! You're a dangerous man, Inspector. I suspect you of being rather good at isolating people's failings. The question is, of course, how good are you at isolating your own?' And with that, he turned away and resumed his trudging walk, up and down, up and down, without offering any further conversation.

Chapter 15

After lunch, Proby called for a general assembly of everyone in the house at the foot of the stairs, so that he could address them easily. Chairs were brought for Sir Thomas, and the Colonel, and Dolly Clare, who was looking pale and shaken. Nanny Fisk indignantly refused to sit down.

'You must all,' he said, watching their upturned faces, some intrigued, others, like Humphrey for example, seemingly bored, 'be aware that we are temporarily marooned in this house. For some reason the police helicopter has not yet come back, although I do still expect it at any time. It might, I suppose, be possible for one of my officers to try to get through to Hampton by swimming, but I don't feel able to take the risk and I also need every available help here.' He was acutely conscious of Emily's intense gaze, her eyes glowing up at him. 'I propose therefore that we sit it out for another day or so. The waters will go down, and I shall then have to ask all of you to remain here until our teams have gathered all the necessary evidence.'

No reaction. Sir Thomas was watching him with a sort of grim satisfaction. Was he perhaps happy temporarily to hand over the seigneurial role to Proby, looming above them on the staircase while amusing himself with the reflection that every dog has its day, however brief?

'In the meantime, I should like to ask you to refrain from going about alone.' This time there was a definite reaction, a sort of collective *shiver.* 'That applies to all of you. I should like to establish the Saloon and the kitchen as the two areas for people to congregate other than for carrying out essential tasks.' He caught Rootham's cynical smile. It was true! He, Proby, was perpetuating the class divide. He'd gone native! No matter. This was a working household, and in Rome, he had decided to accept the Imperial code. 'If and when you leave either,' he added, 'it should be as a pair. What did you say, Captain Humphrey?'

'I said it sounds like a game we used to play called *wolves.* One had a home, but away from that, one was vulnerable. But what,' his voice sank to a dramatic whisper; 'if one's pair is a *wolf*?' No one laughed, and after a while they dispersed in thoughtful silence.

'Let's go through it all again,' said Rootham wearily.

'You lead.' Proby leant back in his chair, and half closed his eyes.

'First question: are the two murders related? Wayne?'

DC Allan cleared his throat. 'For my money, Lady Hatton was killed for her cash. That puts the son and daughter in the frame, along with the old codger and Miss Clare.'

'It's a pity we can't see the actual Will itself,' murmured Proby.

'Don't forget the other beneficiaries,' put in Oates, shyly aggressive in his embarrassment at having to interrupt. 'Miss Weissweiller and Maurice. Any one of them could be on their uppers.'

Rootham nodded. 'We can check their banks when the telephones are back on. There's no hurry. I hope.' He paused. 'I agree with Allan. There was no other reason for Lady Hatton to be killed.'

'So long as we believe the Colonel,' muttered Allan. 'Do we know if the tart had any money?'

Proby shook his head. 'We won't know that till someone gets through. My guess is she had a great deal, but that it won't benefit anyone here.'

'Unless she left it back to Sir Thomas.'

Rootham sat up. 'There's a thought! What if he's

worried about his wife leaving, and Mrs R. too? But I just don't see him as a killer No way!' He lounged back, discouraged.

'I think,' said Proby carefully, 'that there are quite a few possible motives for killing Mrs Roberts.'

'To silence her?'

'That certainly. Though she was supposed to be tucked up with Sir Thomas.'

'If she'd gone to the toilet, she might have met Humphrey coming back with bloodstains?' Allan was looking excited.

'Then why,' growled Oates, 'didn't she say so at once?'

'She's in league with him.'

'With *Humphrey*?'

'It's possible.' Allan, having posed the idea, was sticking to it.

'Or blackmailing him?' mused Proby.

'I like that!' said Rootham. 'The biter bit! He certainly had opportunity for both crimes. Seen in that light, I'd say he's our best chance.'

'Do we think the murder weapon being carried through to the nurse's bedroom was deliberate, to make us think the murderer fled down, or up, the red stairs, or a blind, to disguise the fact that he or she, escaped via the gallery?' Proby had closed his eyes again while speaking.

'Come again?' Oates was looking totally foxed.

'Think about it. There's a dead woman in one room. You've struck her down. On the face of it, you've been remarkably lucky in that she hasn't sprayed blood all over you. Now's the time to get away. You're holding the door-stop. Why do you carry it next door, and then drop it?'

There was silence while they all thought, apart from the buffeting of the rain against the window-panes.

'Here I am, going out,' said Rootham, 'holding the weapon, which I'm going to wash and hide, when I hear someone coming up the staircase. I'm embarrassed to be found holding a bloodstained door-stop, so I put it down.'

'And go out to meet the person? Because no one admits seeing anyone else on the stairs.'

'No. I wait until they've passed.'

'And then go out, leaving it behind?'

'I know,' said Oates excitedly. 'What if that was when the lights failed? That would have given chummy a nasty shock. He mightn't have wanted to spend the rest of the night feeling around for the door-stop. So he panicked and left it behind!'

Proby nodded. 'I think that's certainly one possibility.'

'I prefer the deliberate placing,' said Allan. 'It's *meant* to make us think he went by the red stairs. My money's on Humphrey, tiptoeing down the gallery.'

'And meeting Mrs Roberts?'

They all looked at the floor. It was possible, but unconvincing.

Suddenly Proby stood up. 'I'm going to talk to Maurice,' he said. 'I don't feel I've got behind his "perfect butler" bit yet. I want you to keep mulling it over. We'll get there through the evidence once we can analyse it. But we're more likely to get a conviction if we can trap them first.'

'Who do you think it is?' said Rootham.

Proby stared out of the window. 'I don't know. The lawyer is scared of something. We'll give him a few more hours to stew, and then push him hard. Agreed?' They all nodded.

He found Maurice polishing some silver in the pantry next to the kitchen. The smell of the flood water was much stronger now, with a foul suggestion of sewage about it too. There was even a broad patch of damp spreading below one of the barred windows, evidence that the water-table had risen during the day and was beginning to encroach.

'I'd like to speak to Maurice alone.' Edward, who was sitting perched on the draining-board, reading an old newspaper, got up and went out without comment, closing the door discreetly behind him. Maurice continued to polish the silver, in this case a large rose-bowl with traces of the underlying copper glinting through the silver plate.

'I haven't had a chance to talk to you properly yet,' began Proby. The butler did not look up. 'I would value your opinion.' The slightest of spasms quivered across the mournful bloodless face, to which the lips, pursed now, presented such a striking contrast. In fact, thought Proby, studying the man more carefully, it was the extreme pallor of his complexion that made the lips seem almost carmine. They were moist, and finely formed, and decidedly strange. Taken with the hooded dark eyes, whose gaze was still fixed on the tiny patch of filigree to which he was applying repeated pressure with both thumbs, and the shiny black curls that tightly clustered round the sides and back of his bare dome, they formed a whole head of quite extraordinary distinction.

'How long have you worked here?'

'Forty-seven years, sir.'

'Your parents lived nearby?'

'My father worked the saw-mill.'

'I believe Mrs Roberts's family lived here too.'

The thumbs paused in their work, then resumed, in a slower rhythm.

'I see from my officer's notes that you were born in nineteen thirty-two?'

'That's right.'

'You've never married?' This time the head turned, and Proby was shocked to find himself transfixed by the fierce glare in the butler's eyes. Beneath his professional passivity lurked a character capable of strong reactions, however banked down.

'No, Inspector.' His voice was level, ironic.

'Mrs Roberts, Violet Moore as she then was, was born the year you started here.' No response. 'So you must have seen her about the place.' He paused for inspiration, thinking back to his own childhood, in the shadow of the gaunt stone Castle at Goonby-in-Farthingdale, his own particular Garden of Eden. 'Weren't there Christmas parties in those days?'

This time he had scored. The butler's face lit up. 'Indeed there were! Wonderful parties. All the estate folk, and the kiddies too. Sir Thomas used to have a great fir cut and brought up to the house. Covered in candles it was. Pretty as a picture. The most beautiful sight I ever saw.'

'In the Dining Room?'

'No! At the foot of the stairs. The choirboys would sing carols on the landing, and Her Ladyship would dole out the presents to the mothers and children.'

'To your mother?'

'Of course.' Said with such simple pride.

'And to Violet?'

Silence.

'And to Violet?' Proby persisted.

Maurice bent his head over the rose-bowl and resumed his thumb-work. If this went on, they'd need a new one.

'Please answer my question.'

Maurice sniffed. 'The Moore family were there with all the others.'

'Including Violet?'

The butler shrugged. 'Yes.'

'Mrs Roberts told me that she first remembered talking to Sir Thomas when she was ten, that would be around nineteen fifty-eight. Why would she not have spoken to him when she was, say, eight?'

Again the head turned and regarded him, this time with a look of contemptuous irony. 'I really couldn't say, sir.'

'You mean she was too young before to react to him in a particular way. But surely he would still make an impact on a child. I mean, her father's landlord, the squire, all that sort of thing?'

Maurice scowled, but said nothing. At last he put down the rose-bowl, wiped it methodically with a yellow duster and placed it in a separate collection of completed items.

Proby folded his arms, and lounged against the draining-board. 'When did the Christmas parties cease?'

'*1961.*'

The savage tone of the reply, and its precision, took Proby aback. 'Really? Why?'

Maurice was obviously in the throes of some violent internal debate. Whatever the arguments on either side, candour won the day. 'There was an ugly scene. Old Mr Moore suddenly started shouting out that Sir Thomas had mistreated his daughter She was only thirteen and people were very upset.'

'At the Christmas party?

'Yes, sir. Just as Her Ladyship was presenting the turkeys.'

'And where was Sir Thomas?'

'I don't know, sir.'

'He wasn't there, though?'

'No.'

'Nor Violet?'

A flicker of a smile. 'No, sir.'

'In fact, they were upstairs?'

'So it appeared, sir.'

It must have been quite a scandal. He could imagine the great space, thronged with supplicants. Estate staff, tenants, wives, children. Some grateful, others resentful, but all there, drawn by the need to conform to a community law. And then suddenly, an old man's cracked voice, accusing their master of statutory rape!

'What happened?'

'Nothing.'

Of course. He should have known the answer to that himself, thirty years ago. 'Mr Moore?'

'He retired. I think they settled somewhere north of York.' He was starting on a cream-jug now.

'And Violet?'

'She went to live in Hampton.'

'She must have been still at school?'

'I really couldn't say, sir.'

'When did she return here?'

The butler had put down the cream-jug and was rubbing the back of his neck. 'She never rightly went away.'

'Who killed her?' Proby had been working towards this moment, trying to break down the man's defences.

Maurice's face went completely blank, and he passed his tongue, twice, over his lips. 'It's a puzzle,' he said, showing a reluctant interest.

'Did you ever sleep with her?'

The butler gave no sign at all of hearing the question. 'That is Sir Thomas's bell now, sir. I must go to him.'

He was already out of the room before Proby remembered that the bells, without electricity, were out of action.

Chapter 16

He stayed leaning where he was, staring down into the big enamel sink, into the dark recesses of its plug-hole.

Try as he might to concentrate on the case his mind churned and vibrated, full of thoughts of Emily. How could he have allowed himself to get distracted by a woman? Yes, she was pretty, but so were many women. As for Sheila ... But his mind abruptly veered away from thinking of his wife. It was as if it were programmed to blank out any reference to her. He could only think of Emily, of a quality of yielding softness about her, a fragrance half imagined, half desired. His physical need for her was stifling him. But how or why? There were attractive women everywhere, with whom to be intimate would have physically revolted him. What was the peculiar property of *Emily* that made him hunger for her? Was it just this damned house?

Boyce! The one person in the house showing the classic symptoms of guilt. 'I must go and speak to him,' he thought through a haze of images, Emily undressing, Emily on her back ...

'You're *here*!' She had brought down his clothes and was standing in the doorway.

He stared down at her, his body noting each part of hers, his expression matching hers in a tentative, puzzled, even frightened hunger for passion.

'*Inspector*!' Rootham was standing in the doorway, glowering.

'Yes?' Proby glowered back, without moving.

'It's the lawyer. They've found his body in the garden. He's just killed himself.'

Chapter 17

The body was sprawled across three of the curved steps leading down from the garden door There was no blood, but the skull was hideously deformed by the impact and one eye, dislodged by this, bulged out beyond his nose, staring up at them in a dreadful wild reproach. Oates had been standing inside the locked door when the lawyer's body had plummeted onto the top step outside, less than four feet from him.

Gusts of heavy rain slanted down on them, both on the dead man and on the four subdued policemen grouped about him, yet none of them noticed, so engrossed were they all in their own thoughts.

After a few minutes of examining the body while Rootham photographed it with a camera borrowed from Miss Weissweiller, Proby reluctantly gave the order for it to be covered, and then carried indoors.

Mrs Freeman had brought them a heavy dustsheet, and with this in place, Proby and Rootham took the legs, and Allan and Oates the arms. Shouldering the body, no easy task, they bore their burden back up the steps and through the garden doors, held open by Maurice and Edward. Giving him a pomp in death he would have so appreciated in life, they crossed the hall with heavy tread and began the long ascent up the great stairs.

In the hall they had passed Sir Thomas, his head bowed, with John and Emily beside him. Dolly Clare, her face quivering, stood in the Morning Room doorway opposite, leaning painfully on the old Colonel's arm.

Then, as the procession turned to approach the stairs, Mrs Freeman and Miss Weissweiller, the former carrying a second blanket, watched them pass without expression. No one spoke.

Up they climbed, past the statues, and past the squat menacing figure of Nanny Fisk, halted on the landing to let them pass.

'*Hello*! What's this? *Charades*?'

Captain Humphrey had burst through the door from the upper gallery. He was very drunk indeed. He stared, and then started giggling.

'Out of the way, Captain Humphrey!'

It was all they could do to get past him, and the fumes of whisky were overwhelming. The man stank!

Down the upper Gallery the solemn cortège proceeded until at last, with very considerable relief, they were able to pitch the dead lawyer onto his bed. It sagged under the weight in death, as it must also have done in life.

'He's a bloody ton,' sighed Allan, rubbing his arms to restore the circulation.

'Now,' said Proby. 'We'll go up and see where he went over. Oates, you search the room. Allan, you check where everybody was at the time.'

'I'll show you.' The way to the roof was via the landing that also led to John and Emily Hatton's rooms at the top of the blue staircase, and she was standing there when they reached the foot of the stairs.

With mixed feelings, Proby followed her up, with Rootham dogging his heels.

'This is my room.' As if by chance she had manoeuvred him into a low chamber in which the narrow bed, upholstered in a bright red and green chintz, was, for him, the most significant feature. The window did, as he had seen from the forecourt, start at floor level and reach up only to about the level of the wash-basin, a heavy price to pay for uniformity in the house's façade.

'And the roof?' called Rootham, impatiently.

'This way.' There were three other doors leading from the landing: her brother's room, their bathroom, and a narrow door, with thick plain hinges shaped like brackets, which opened to reveal precipitous wooden steps.

Emily bounded up these, with the others climbing awkwardly after her. The woodwork smelt damp, and slightly smoky, and at the top, another narrow door let them out onto the flat roof of the house.

'Bloody hell!' The gale blew his words away. Squat chimney stacks all round them emitted thin wisps of flying smoke, lowered no doubt to hide their presence. On the massive balustrading, stone lions, four, five times life size, strutted and crouched, preserving, at this great height, their proper perspective for mere mortals at ground level.

There was only one point where the leaded platform of the roof rose so that a man could step onto the balustrade without an awkward climb, and that was via a recently repaired stepped construction which appeared to house some kind of industrial-sized ratchet and chain. Approaching this with great caution, Proby peered over the unprotected parapet. They were immediately above the garden steps.

'THIS IS THE PLACE!' he shouted at Rootham, who nodded. For half an hour they searched the leads, methodically covering every fold and crevice. They found nothing to give the slightest clue as to why the lawyer had plunged to his death, whether by choice, or by a treacherous push.

Coming down the staircase, they reached their own rooms, leading through into Proby's own state bedroom. 'What happens further down?' he said, suddenly. 'There must be two rooms on the mezzanine.'

'Miss Weissweiller and Nanny Fisk,' said Oates, who had rejoined them, having found nothing in the dead lawyer's room. 'I'm over the latter. You should hear her snore!' He was no mean contributor himself.

'I should like to speak to Miss Weissweiller first,' said Proby. 'I can't believe Boyce would have walked through our rooms.'

'Here?'

'No. Downstairs.'

'The Justice Room?' They were all catching it now. Soon they'd be putting on stiff collars!

'The Incident Room,' he said firmly, and went back to his room for a clean handkerchief.

Waiting for Miss Weissweiller, he noted down the reports of others' movements. Mrs Freeman, John Hatton and Nanny Fisk were all in the clear; they had been together looking through some old photographs in the Estate Office. Sir Thomas had been in his room, the Colonel had been in the toilet and Miss Weissweiller had been checking cutlery in the Dining Room. Captain Humphrey and Dolly Clare, who had burst into tears twice during their short conversation, reported having met each other on the great staircase. Maurice had been in the basement decanting some wine for dinner and Edward had been out stoking the boiler. No one seemed to have paid much attention to his advice about sticking together.

'You heard no one climbing your stairs?'

'No one.' Miss Weissweiller was watching him through her thick spectacles, her face a mask of superior disinterest. 'I cannot help you.'

'It's surprising how little details help,' said Proby with a bland smile, which was not returned. 'You've worked here for, I think, eighteen years?'

'That is so.'

'And before that?'

'I worked for Sir Thomas in his property company.'

'How did you come to work there?'

'How?' She didn't seem to understand the question.

'Your name. I assumed you were German.'

'You assumed wrong then,' she said. 'My grandfather was Swiss, but my parents lived in Castlewick. I got my first job in the Hatton Estates Company when I left secretarial college, and I've worked for Sir Thomas ever since.'

'Is he a good employer?'

She tossed her head. 'That is a ridiculous question, Inspector. I should hardly still be here if I did not enjoy my work.'

'I suppose not.' She did not look like a woman who would suffer indignities. Yet she had made up their beds when the daily housemaids couldn't come into work. And, since he had never seen her exchange a word with anyone else during these two days, he felt that she must be very lonely.

'I was told that you were the most likely person to tell me who is behind these murders,' he tried.

'Then you took a very long time before consulting me,' she snapped.

He looked up, suddenly alert. There was a satisfaction in her voice, smugness, malice even, which seemed to herald a revelation. 'You mean you know who is responsible?'

'Of *course.*' Her self-confidence was striking.

'Please tell me.'

'The Devil!' His heart sank. 'The Evil One, who spitteth his venom into the bowels of Men. This is not a house of God! But He will overcome.'

'But –'

'Vengeance is mine, saith the Lord. I will repay!'

'Who –'

'Even as Beelzebub creepeth among the little ones ...' It was no good. She was well and truly under way, and it took him another ten minutes to extricate himself from her diatribe. Still, there was one interesting conclusion. Sir Thomas's own suspicion of 'Evil' might have arisen from long association with this fanatic. He resolved to speak again to his host as soon as he had braved an encounter with Nanny Fisk.

But in this he was frustrated, for he was told that she had gone to bed, bolting her door against the casual intrusions of stray policemen, and announcing that she would not descend again until it was time for her breakfast, at seven-thirty sharp the following morning.

Chapter 18

The casual search of Mrs Roberts's and John Boyce's rooms having yielded nothing of interest, the policemen ate early before taking up their stations for another night of watching. More oil lamps had been dug out from the backs of old cupboards and unused storerooms, so that every corridor in the house was now lit, more or less adequately. The servants all retired as soon as dinner in the Dining Room had been cleared away, even Maurice admitting that he was quite exhausted.

Nor was there much impetus for gaiety among the others. The old Colonel and Miss Clare retired immediately, ignoring Captain Humphrey's persistent calls for a rubber of 'how's-your-father'. Sir Thomas retired alone to his office, at the foot of the red staircase, saying he had some paperwork to deal with.

John Hatton and Humphrey spent a stale half-hour, quarrelling over two hands of picquet. Then they, too, reluctantly rose and left Emily alone in the empty room, staring at her book.

Impulsively she stood up, threw it down and went out into the hall. It was empty, except for Rootham, lounging on a wicker armchair he had carried up to the main stairs' landing.

'Where is Inspector Proby?' she asked.

He glared at her. 'He's having a rest,' he said repressively. 'And writing to his wife.'

'Thank you so much,' she said sweetly, before walking past him and up towards the Gallery. Sourly, he watched her turn right towards the Inspector's room. Women!

She tapped on the door.

'Who is it?'

'May I come through?'

He came to the door, tousled, his shirt half undone. 'What is it?'

'Do you mind if I come through your room? It's the quickest way to my room, and I'm frightened about going back down through the corridor.' She was conscious that Rootham had followed her, was standing listening.

'Yes, do,' said Proby, standing aside to let her past.

'Give me five minutes,' she whispered. 'And then come up.'

'A word, Inspector!' It was Rootham, persistent as any hunt terrier.

'Come on!' said Proby brusquely. They both watched Emily across the room and, with something of a wiggle, exit through the further door. 'What?'

'I'm tired. I want you to take my place for the next two hours.'

Proby stared at him. 'What are you talking about? I've never seen anyone fresher!'

'Nevertheless ...' Rootham's expression was truculent. 'That's my formal request. Sir.'

'Why?'

'If you want it in plain bloody English, to stop you making a fool of yourself.'

Proby's face flushed. 'You mean ...?'

'Yes." Rootham's face was red too. Embarrassment or anger?

'What business is it of yours?' Proby towered over him, suddenly menacing.

Rootham drew a hand over his forehead. 'None' he said, in a tired voice. 'It's no business of mine except,' angrily, 'that I'm your friend.'

'And you know what I've had to put up with Sheila. You know about her lovers.'

'I know you love her,' said Rootham simply.

'What about that young nurse? You screwed her all

round the houses without a second thought.'

'Yes,' shouted Rootham. 'That's the bloody *point.* If you weren't so dense, you'd see it for yourself. *I* can do that, because I don't give it another thought. But you! You're not like that. You go to bed with this girl, you'll agonize about it. I know you. And in the end you'll spoil it all by confessing to Sheila. Maybe she doesn't give a damn. Maybe even she'd like you to have a fling, because that'd make her feel less guilty. But you go and tell her, and you'll spoil seventeen years of good marriage for yourself, and for her. And that's how it'd be. I know you.'

'Good marriage!' Proby hardly knew if he was standing or sitting.

'Of course. Can't you see how all the others envy you? Sheila loves you. She's not a saint, but, good God, she's the wife for you, and you know it!'

Proby grumbled something inarticulate and wiped his forehead.

'It isn't going anywhere,' Rootham said softly. 'And when it ends, you'll be hurt, and you'll hurt both of them too. There's a balance. The more pleasure, the more pain. Spare them the pain, Jim.'

Proby sat up. 'You're right,' he said dully. 'Fetch that bottle of whisky over there and a couple of glasses. Perhaps we'll find peace instead. This *bloody* house!' But his eyes, fixed on Rootham's retreating back, were bleak indeed.

Chapter 19

When he woke in the morning, it was to hear that Sir Thomas was planning a general expedition to the church, this having been his invariable routine on a Sunday morning since his childhood.

Proby saw no reason not to agree to this, with the sole proviso that everyone must attend except DC Allan who would guard the house. He returned to his room to fetch a notebook, and was immediately reminded of Emily's last whispered words. No wonder she had looked a wreck this morning, scarcely deigning to meet his smiled greeting.

As for Rootham, sitting staring out over the flooded gardens, his thoughts were turned sourly onto his career prospects. Proby might thank him for his interference. Alternatively, he might never forgive him. Why on earth hadn't he let the man do what he wanted and screw the girl? What was so wrong with that? And he, Rootham, could get on with his own life, minding his own bloody business. For that matter, why shouldn't they take a little pleasure from this dreadful episode in their lives?

He blew his nose angrily, and went back to counting seconds until he was due to join the church party, for whom Edward had laid out a prodigious selection of wellington boots in the hall.

They were just about to set off when John Hatton took Proby on one side.

'I'm sorry to bother you, Inspector,' he said, 'but something rather odd happened early this morning.'

'Tell me.'

'I went out for a walk, or should I say a paddle. With your constable's permission, of course.' He was fiddling with his cigarette holder. Perhaps Sir Thomas discouraged smoking before church? 'I happened to be looking at the house, and I could have sworn I saw someone in poor Boyce's bedroom. But your constable says it's all sealed up. I thought I should tell you.'

Proby considered this with his head on one side. 'Thank you,' he said, and summoning Rootham, he told him to supervise a further, closer search of all three victims' rooms. If someone was willing to risk being caught in such incriminating circumstances, there must be something worth looking for.

It was an experience for all of them, splashing through the shallows on the terrace under umbrellas, chilled by the gusts of rain and wind, to find Maurice still struggling to open the chapel door with a chisel.

'Let me.' Rootham took out a bunch of small but weirdly shaped instruments from his trouser pocket and had the door swinging open in less than a minute.

Sir Thomas appeared, escorted by Edward from among the topiary, a strangely impressive figure in his old-fashioned brown bowler hat and wearing his habitual expression of grim irony.

He took his place at what must normally have been the Vicar's desk, for he could hardly see over it, and stared fixedly round at the unusual congregation. 'Let us pray!'

All about them lay the tombs and memorials and hatchments of past Hattons, here the marble image of a crusader knight, his hands carved in everlasting marble supplication, his armoured feet warmed by twin alabaster hounds, there on the wall the arms of the first Sir Thomas, bearing in pretence the arms of his second wife, heiress to much of the land still held south of the river. Above the chancel arch loomed a heavy oak lozenge, emblazoned in glorious technicolour with the elaborate achievement of the present Sir Thomas's mother, last of her line, bringing no less than thirty-two quarterings into the family.

The message conveyed seemed more of family pride than of Christian humility. And yet, thought Proby, amused to see a glowing representation of the baroque Abbey standing four-square in the background of an eighteenth-century stained-glass crucifixion, surely this craftsmanship was all dedicated to, and inspired by, a wish to beautify their place of worship.

'We mourn the untimely passing of three members of this congregation: Florence Emily Witherspoon Hatton, Violet Elizabeth Roberts, and John Zeberdee Boyce.' Sir Thomas paused. How many men, having lost both their wife and their mistress in the space of two days, could have handled such an event with calm, even aplomb? He lifted up his voice: 'We commend their souls to Almighty God. Grant them eternal rest, O Lord, and may light perpetual shine upon them!'

'AMEN!' This from old Colonel Fetherstonehaugh, in a fruity tone. Someone was sobbing. Dolly Clare? It certainly wasn't Emily, who was watching Proby impassively, nor John Hatton, who seemed mesmerized by his grandmother's coat-of-arms. Proby, looking round, was amazed to catch a *smile* on Maurice's face, hastily erased.

A thought suddenly struck Proby as he looked round at all the family embellishments. Were the Hattons themselves any less of a gang than the *boys-in-blue*? Individually they might, like most individuals, be more or less polite, co-operative and weak. But place them in a group, whether four contemporaries dressed up as policemen, or thirty generations over eight hundred years dressed up in heraldry, and the strength (with its attendant insolence) of *belonging* became theirs.

'... and her light was like unto a stone most precious, even like a jasper stone, clear as crystal ...' Sir Thomas's voice echoed gravely round the little church, so modest in its dimensions as to make its towering domestic neighbour seem the very personification of Mammon. '...And there shall be no night there; and they need no candle, neither the light of the sun; for the Lord God giveth them light: and they shall reign for ever and ever.' The old man slammed the book shut. 'Let us pray.'

After the service was over, Sir Thomas, yielding up his brown bowler to Edward as they climbed back up the steps to the house, invited Proby to join him for a cup of coffee. As he spoke, they were crossing the very spot where Boyce's body had lain the day before, though the rain had long washed away any stain.

'I'd like that,' replied Proby politely, sending Rootham off for the renewed search.

Maurice brought them a tray of coffee and they sat for a while, sipping the hot liquid, companionably silent.

'I am rather *assuming*,' said Sir Thomas cautiously, 'that John Boyce must have been responsible for my wife's murder.' He paused. When Proby did not respond, he added: 'And that of Mrs Roberts.'

'Why so?' enquired Proby.

'Well.' The old man seemed momentarily nonplussed. 'It seems likely, doesn't it? He did commit suicide, after all. That's why I wanted to talk this through with you.'

'What did you and Boyce discuss yesterday after I left you?'

'I?' queried the baronet. 'With Boyce?'

'As I left, you asked me to send for Maurice. Later I met Mr Boyce going upstairs. I can't see why Maurice would conceal that you sent him to summon Boyce here, if that is what you did.'

The old man smiled. 'Of course not. It's no secret. I did send for Boyce. I need to remake my own will, now that two of the principal beneficiaries are dead.'

'I thought you and your wife had agreed not to leave property to each other.'

Another smile. He could almost see the man's mind computing his next move. 'We *agreed* that certainly. But I had no intention whatever of abiding by that. There are a number of personal items that I would always have bequeathed to my wife, simply to gratify my wish to pay public honour to her. Now I must make other dispositions.'

'I see.'

'He did, however say something rather strange.'

'Yes?'

'We had finished discussing my new Will, which really was pretty simple, and he was leaving for the door, when he suddenly paused. Then he turned round, and said, "Whatever may happen, Sir Thomas, I want you to believe I never meant to hurt you." I wanted to call him back, to demand an explanation, but he just blundered out of the room. He was quite a foolish man in some ways. But an obedient servant.'

'Had you not considered that his death might have been murder?' asked Proby quietly.

'Murder? On the *roof*?' scoffed the old man. 'Not even Boyce would allow himself to be pushed off a roof! No.' He resumed his grave contemplative manner. 'I think you will find that, for reasons we shall never know, Boyce killed himself on realizing that he was about to be found out. Incredible as it seems.'

'Incredible,' echoed Proby.

'I think you'll find my daughter Emily agrees,' said the old man silkily. 'Talk it over with her. She may change your mind.'

There was a knock on the door.

'Well?' Sir Thomas was clearly furious at being interrupted.

It was Rootham, who came in, holding a piece of paper. 'I thought you should see this, sir. Concealed in the lawyer's room. I can't think how we didn't think to look there before.'

Proby took it. It was Lady Hatton's Will.

Chapter 20

Watched steadily by his silent host, Proby read twice through the document, which was torn across one corner, and then handed it, without a word, to the baronet.

It was a single sheet of paper, closely typed, and was, in Proby's experience, unusually straightforward and to the point:

> I Florence Emily Witherspoon, Lady Hatton, of Hatton Abbey in the county of Hampton, declare this to be my Last Will and Testament, and hereby revoke all other previous dispositions:
>
> I appoint John Zeberdee Boyce and Peter Brydges to act as my executors, authorizing them to charge to my estate all appropriate fees arising from their acting in their professional capacities and I direct them to clear any outstanding debts and to meet my funeral expenses. Subject to the aforegoing I bequeath:
>
> 1. To my very dear friend Alexander Fetherstonehaugh, one hundred thousand pounds;
> 2. To my dear friend Dorothy Clare, one hundred thousand pounds;
> 3. To my son John the freehold, contents and all connected fixtures and fittings of my London property 7, Rutland Gate, SW7, this bequest to be free of estate duty;
> 4. To my daughter Emily all such US securities and company stock as I may be possessed of at my death;
> 5. To Amelia Weissweiller and Maurice Bourke five thousand pounds each free of estate duty providing that they be still in my family's employ at my death;
> 6. The residue of my estate I leave to be divided as to

two thirds to my elder son Frederick, and as to one third to my younger son John.

It was signed in a straggling hand, witnessed by John Zeberdee Boyce and Violet Elizabeth Roberts, and dated Thursday, the day she had died.

Sir Thomas had leant over to read the document closely, but Proby suddenly realized that the old man had bent still further, seemed indeed to be in danger of tipping right out of his chair.

'Are you all right, sir?' He touched the other's arm. For a dreadful moment there was no response.

Then, very slowly, the old man righted himself. His face had changed colour to a muddy grey.

Proby jumped up and crossed to the cupboard where he seen John Hatton refill his glass. There was a line of bottles and glasses inside, and he poured two inches of brandy into a glass and hurried back.

Sir Thomas gulped the drink, coughing loudly afterwards. Then he took some more. 'Thank you,' he gasped. 'You can't imagine how it affected me, seeing her handwriting again.'

'You can confirm that that is her signature?'

'Yes indeed!' He seemed to take comfort from his emphatic reply.

They sat for a while in silence, then Proby said, 'There are two inconsistencies here.'

'Really?'

'First, Boyce told me that your wife's Will was in his office in Castlewick, which he must have known was a lie.'

'And the other?' He seemed completely recovered now.

'The dating of the Will. The only reason why Boyce would have lied to me about the Will must have been to conceal, however temporarily, its date.'

'Why do you assume that?'

'Because he told me every other detail quite frankly. There was no suggestion, however, that it was a new Will, let alone one of the day of her death.'

'I see.'

'What I need now, and urgently, is the previous Will.'

'And how would that help?'

'It will reveal in what particular your wife's dispositions have changed.'

'I think,' said Sir Thomas after a pause, 'that I can help there. Originally her residue, which is of course the meat of the matter, was to be split equally between our two surviving sons. Latterly, however she has felt that the cost of keeping this house in order, which will devolve upon my son Frederick, required a larger share of the estate.'

Proby frowned. 'And your elder son? Where is he now?'

'Courting,' said Sir Thomas with a slight smile. 'He has met a young woman who lives in Berwickshire. They seem very much in love.'

'He is staying with her parents?'

Sir Thomas shook his head. 'They are both staying with some relations of hers, near Inverness.'

Proby rose. 'Shall I send Maurice to you?' he enquired.

Sir Thomas shook his head. 'I should prefer to be alone for a while,' he said.

'Is there nothing else you wish to tell me, Sir Thomas?'

'No,' said the old man. And turned his face away towards the fireplace.

Proby closed the door softly. It was time to think, time to get away from the others, to reflect on the whole case. Usually he would have pulled on a coat and gone for a tramp through the park. Barred by the floods, he decided to follow his host's example, so made his way up to the upper Gallery. There, hands clasped behind his back, he proceeded to pace, all afternoon, up and down, up and down, until Oates, who was still searching Lady Hatton's rooms, was thoroughly sick of it.

Then, at half past six, his expression less troubled perhaps than it had been for two days, he walked round to the Saloon through the Dining Room, in order to avoid disturbing Sir Thomas, and asked Dolly Clare if she would join him in the Incident Room.

'Do you need me?' asked the old Colonel, suddenly made anxious at the change in her expression. Her legs seemed barely able to support her, let alone cross the room. Indeed she had visibly shrunk during the last two days, and had exchanged that rosy-cheeked vigour for a drawn and sunken look of despair. Perhaps the deaths had served to alert him uncomfortably to the natural but inevitable approach of her own.

'No, thank you, my dear,' she replied, unsteadily. 'I'll be back soon.'

But she wasn't, and at eight o'clock a message from the Inspector was circulated, asking that everyone should join the Inspector in the Saloon. Edward even brought up some fresh, if damp, logs in honour of what he thought might be a long evening.

It was as Proby was preparing for this assembly, checking some figures as he sat at the desk in the estate office that, suddenly, something very shocking happened. The telephone rang.

It was so unexpected that Proby actually jumped. For three days he had lived without that most ordinary of daily sounds. And those three days had so reconditioned his brain that now it seemed a monstrous intrusion.

'Detective Inspector Proby, please.'

'Speaking.' It was Dorothy, the Chief Constable's amanuensis.

'Oh, Mr Proby. I have the Chief Constable for you.'

'Thank you.' He made a face at the empty room, screwing up his lips and making goggling movements with his eyes.

'James? Have we really finally got you?'

'Yes, sir.'

'We've had an absolutely dreadful time. I'd have sent the helicopter to get you all if there'd been even a moment. It's always the same when Rankin's away. How are things? I must say you're in the right place.'

'I'm sorry?'

'Well, living it up among the fleshpots while the rest of us have to slave away. We've got most of the flooded people evacuated. Rufus Down had a Red Alert after one of the compressor chambers flooded, and we had to evacuate the whole complex! At least the forecasters say the waters will go down now, whether the rain continues or not.'

'I see.'

'You don't sound very interested.'

'I could do with some assistance this end, sir. If you can spare it.'

'Oh? I meant to ask, what happened to Lady Hatton? Heart attack, that sort of thing, was it?' So he'd never really take it seriously either.

'She was murdered.'

'*What?*'

'In fact.' said Proby, taking a deep breath, 'three people have died. I need Forensic, a full scene-of-crime squad, Dr Milligan and the Home Office team as soon as you can let me have them. Perhaps the helicopter ...?'

'*Three* dead?' In a whisper.

'I'm afraid so.'

'Not Sir Thomas?'

'No, sir. Sir Thomas is fine.'

'Any leads?' Disbelieving.

'Yes, sir. This line is not secure. But I need the back-up for evidence. I have identified the probable murderer.' Somewhere, quite close, he thought he heard a footfall.

'It's … um … eight o'clock now. I'll have them there first thing … say eight o'clock tomorrow?'

'Thank you, sir.'

'*Three dead*!' The Chief rang off. Proby could imagine the news spreading through the Headquarters building.

Immediately he dialled his home number. There was no reply.

Slowly, reluctantly, he turned away and started to walk towards the Saloon, the same room where he had first seen them all together. The task ahead was not one that he relished, even though the crimes had been despicable. And as he walked, his footfalls echoed on the marble, steady as a drumbeat, harbinger of doom.

Chapter 21

There they all were, grouped around the room like characters in a West End play.

Sir Thomas sat now behind his desk, his face set in its characteristically stern expression. John, his son, leant against the mantelpiece, a glass of brandy in one hand, and the eternal cigarette in its holder in the other.

Old Colonel Fetherstonehaugh was sitting bolt upright but nodding gently in the wing chair beside the fireplace. Was he really asleep, or just pretending?

Miss Weissweiller and Nanny Fisk, sat, like furious bookends, fuming at either end of the big sofa, both staring straight in front of them with hands folded in their laps, while Captain Humphrey, impervious to the atmosphere on either side of him, lounged in the middle of the sofa, playing with his tie. Dolly Clare had been brought in last by Rootham and helped to a chair drawn up beside Sir Thomas. Hunched there, she was watching his face anxiously, while Emily, her eyes as ever fixed on Proby, was perched on the fire-seat, one hand dangled elegantly to catch what little heat Edward's damp logs might emit. Maurice and Edward stood discreetly by the two doors, as if unaware of the other police officers posted outside.

'It seems,' drawled John Hatton, 'that we are all assembled.' He drew delicately on his cigarette and blew a perfect ring towards the ceiling. 'I hope this won't take long. I'm *aching* for dinner!'

'Mrs Freeman?' growled Sir Thomas, looking round.

'She was worried about the cooking, being all on her own,' said Proby. 'I said we wouldn't be needing her.'

'Very good of you.' It sounded bland, but carried a distinct rebuke. Mrs Freeman took her orders from Sir

Thomas, as did everyone in the room apart from the Inspector.

'Now that our investigation is over,' said Proby, 'and as we shall be departing tomorrow now that the floods are going down, I thought I should tell all of you the truth of what happened here this weekend.'

'Quite right,' said the Colonel.

'Spiffing!' mimicked Humphrey, drawing fresh waves of loathing upon himself.

'I must say that I have not been helped by the deliberate concealment that most of you have practised in one form or another, and which seriously hampered our efforts.'

He looked round sternly, but no one, except Emily, her eyes smudged with fatigue, met his gaze.

'Lady Hatton's murder could have been carried out by any one of you. I made some tentative guesses at how that happened, almost all of which were wrong. But the Colonel here was absolutely right in his suggestion that the motive there was money. More or less.' He paused and rubbed his eyes. He was pretty tired himself, now it was all over.

'The murder of Mrs Roberts, however, changed the perspective. This could not have been for gain. It must therefore have been either to silence her as a witness, or as an accomplice. Both crimes were marked by a casual violence and cruelty which I and my officers find very repugnant.'

Miss Weissweiller was nodding her head vigorously. 'Disgusting!' she said. Someone giggled, instantly suppressing the sound.

'At first I thought that only John Boyce, Captain Humphrey or Sir Thomas could have been the culprits. However the focus proved to be wider than that. My assumptions were based on the fact that I had an officer watching both the main stairs and the ground floor door to the service stairs that led up to Mrs Roberts's suite. I had forgotten that those same service stairs descend to the basement. Anyone on either of the other mezzanine stairs could have descended to the basement using the steps in the Trophy Room, passed through the basement and up the two flights of the service stairs without my officer seeing them. Any one of you, therefore, could have killed Mrs Roberts too. These murders could have been separate, but I believed them to be connected, and in this I was correct.'

He paused to gauge their reactions. The old Colonel had certainly woken up, was watching him intently. Dolly Clare was sobbing silently into a large silk handkerchief.

'A number of you had considerable financial expectations from Lady Hatton: her son and daughter, the Colonel here and Miss Clare, as well as Miss Weissweiller and Maurice. There were also particular circumstances which could be said to provide a possible motive both for Sir Thomas and for Mrs Roberts herself. Nor could I rule out the possibility of confederates, whether keeping watch, or actually assisting in the crime.

'Then we had the death of John Boyce. This could have been suicide, although, unusually, he left no note, or it could have been murder. Very few of you had satisfactory alibis at the time that he must have been up on the roof. I had to ask myself under what circumstances a man would allow himself to be lured onto the roof of a building such as this at a time when a double murderer was known to be in the house. I decided there were no such circumstances, and that Mr Boyce's death was indeed suicide. Further, this was only explicable if he had been in some material way involved in the previous murders.'

'There you are, Inspector,' said Sir Thomas. 'Exactly what I said!'

'Not quite,' replied Proby. 'You remember the

promise you extracted from me?' The old man nodded grimly. 'As I shall explain, Boyce was materially involved. But he was far from acting alone.

'The next phenomenon was the discovery of Lady Hatton's new Will, not in his office safe as he had told me, but here hidden in his bedroom, a room we had already searched.

'Because of the unusual way it came to our attention, tipped off by John Hatton of an alleged intruder ...'

'I say ...'

Proby held up one hand, effectively silencing the younger man. 'Moreover there was one remarkable feature about the new Will: *everyone involved in making it was already dead.*

'I therefore had to consider also the possibility that it was a forgery. But these avenues also led nowhere. Our seals on Mr Boyce's bedroom were intact. There had been no intruder, and therefore no planting of the Will either. We had missed it first time through. Moreover comparing the signatures with written materials recovered from the dead persons' own effects established that all three signatures were genuine. The Will was perfectly valid, and not a forgery.

'I had, therefore, to examine the *effect* of the Will. Here I began to run up against a deliberate campaign of sustained untruths. Thinking back, I realize that the terms of this Will, communicated quite openly to me by John Boyce, did indeed come as a surprise, however carefully concealed by him, to Sir Thomas. As soon as I left him, he had Mr Boyce brought before him. It must have been a shattering interview, for I passed Boyce on the stairs after it, and he looked half dead. As indeed he was, for shortly afterwards he climbed onto the roof and threw himself off it to certain death!

'Whatever you said to him, Sir Thomas,' he was facing the grim old face. Sir Thomas's impassive expression never varied. He might have been another of the stone statues on the great stairs, 'and, whatever it was, it certainly didn't concern your own Will, it sent him to his death.

'I think I know what it was, but then I encountered something stranger. When we actually found the Will and I showed it to you, you were overcome. So much so that I believe you were close to suffering a stroke.

'What could have caused that? You knew about the Will, I myself had told you about it, and its terms. So what so shocked you that you nearly died of it?' Sir Thomas's face preserved its stony secrets. 'One thing only was new to you: the identity of the witnesses. It was, I think, only then that you appreciated the full involvement of Violet Roberts in your wife's murder. And I can quite see that that must have been a peculiarly painful shock. Yet even then you did not decrease your efforts to mislead me. Three people were involved. Boyce, I am certain, had no idea originally that a murder was planned, hence his willing acquiescence in what you and he actually talked about immediately before his death: your suggested way out, the ultimate test of his obedience to you.' Still Sir Thomas said nothing. Indeed he appeared not to be listening, his head held immobile, his face retaining a fixed expression of ironic detachment.

'But there had to be a third conspirator. So let us reconstruct the crimes. X, with Boyce and Mrs Roberts as confederates, persuades Lady Hatton to sign a new Will. Mrs Roberts, who has already spent part of the night with Sir Thomas, has left him soundly asleep, happily unaware of her treachery. This, of course, gave her one of the few alibis for that first night. I believe Boyce left Lady Hatton's room after the signing, but the others remained. We may never know what alerted Lady Hatton to wrong-doing. She could scarcely read, but perhaps the presence of Mrs Roberts, hardly the natural choice in the circumstances, led her to scrutinize the Will more carefully after she had signed it. Hence the tear, for it was snatched away from her. We know that a symptom of her distressing illness was to throw off her clothes. It doesn't matter which of the two struck her down, both are guilty. Certainly the survivor, for self-protection or, as I think, sheer malice, returned the second night to strangle Mrs Roberts, the only person who could testify against them.'

'This is a very sustained effort,' said Humphrey, unexpectedly sobered. 'But will you ever get to the point? I'm not sure why you are indulging this unexpected though not unamusing taste for melodrama!' He was not the only member of the audience to be growing restive.

'Because,' said Proby, unperturbed, 'I wish to avenge these two crimes. I needed a final link, and this was provided this evening by Miss Clare.' All eyes turned on the old lady, still sniffing miserably. 'Because of Sir Thomas's deliberate and sustained attempts to mislead me by lying about the details in his wife's original Will, it suddenly struck me that Miss Clare, her oldest friend, was one of the two people in whom she would have been likely to confide. And since the other, Colonel Fetherstonehaugh, seemed not to be nursing any painful secrets, whereas Miss Clare was positively wasting away in front of us with hers, I decided that she was almost certainly protecting someone, and why?' It was a rhetorical question and treated as such by his audience. 'Because Lady Hatton had foreseen her own death, and had persuaded Miss Clare not to betray someone who was dear to her, *even if she was murdered.* A devoted woman indeed. My job this evening was to persuade Miss Clare that more lives might be at risk unless she revealed her two pieces of knowledge.'

'Oh, Tommy!' The old lady had flung herself sobbing at the old man's feet. 'I'm so sorry.' He bent over her and patted her hand. But still he did not speak.

'The first thing she told me was that it had always been Lady Hatton's intention to leave her London house, and its very valuable contents, to her daughter Emily. The new Will removed this provision more than doubling her younger son's inheritance.'

'This is absurd!' John Hatton had put down his brandy glass, his face white with anger. 'Why would I hurt my own mother?'

'Greed,' said Proby. 'Greed, impatience and, I expect, considerable debts.'

'It's ridiculous,' said Hatton, carefully avoiding his father's steady gaze. 'This is all conjecture. This is Grand Guignol without evidence.'

'That is where you are wrong,' said Proby. 'Mrs Roberts gave me one vital piece of information. She said that your mother could barely read *with a magnifying glass*. For some time I attached no importance to a shard of broken glass beside your mother's body. Then I realized what it was. It was a fragment from her magnifying glass. I have no doubt the poor old lady was desperately trying to read the provisions of the new Will you and Boyce had just persuaded her to sign. Yet there was no sign of such a glass anywhere among her effects. It must have been hidden therefore. The second piece of information Miss Clare gave me was where you and she used to play parlour games in the basement. She showed me your favourite hiding place. The glass was there, of course, and we have it ready for examination by our laboratory tomorrow.' He held out the fragments, bagged in plastic.

'It was *her*!' he screamed, as Proby shouted out the formulaic caution. 'John Hatton, I am arresting you ...'

'*It was her idea. She wanted to be Lady Hatton.*'

'You are not obliged to say anything...!'

'*Daddy! Please believe me!*'

'...will be used in evidence against you.'

'*I never meant to hurt her.*' Rootham and the others had burst in when the shouting started, and had him safely under restraint. '*She couldn't wait either!*' If, as was likely, he had worn gloves, this carefully goaded admission was their only chance for a conviction.

Throughout the last few minutes, Sir Thomas's head had never moved. He had seemed more like one of his Eastern carvings, immobile, inscrutable. But the sound of his son's weeping at last produced a reaction, a single gesture of weary disgust.

'You must help him.' The voice, low and vibrating with emotion, was Emily's.

Proby stared at her. 'Help him ...?'

'My father.' So there were things beyond even the great patriarch's capabilities. He wanted the evidence of his son's guilt, his son's presence indeed, removed, but lacked, for once, the stern resolution to give the necessary order.

Three days in this household, so far removed from his own life, had not been entirely wasted. Proby cocked an eye at 'Nero' who, totally impassive like his master throughout the whole humiliating scene, calmly opened the door.

And when it was completed, and his son had been handcuffed and led away, Sir Thomas in a quiet voice, spoke one slow single word, '*Evil!*'

After that, he remained entirely still, his eye apparently fixed upon the centre of the carved mantelpiece opposite. Slowly, reluctantly, the others left him alone, Proby being the last to leave a room where the only sound was now the melancholy hiss of the damp logs, smouldering uselessly in the hearth, and the remorseless ticking of the tall bronze clock that sat, changelessly smug, on the wall-bracket behind his desk.

Chapter 22

The next morning, Proby awoke in the dark, abruptly, panic-stricken. And immediately remembered where he was.

The four-poster. The Tapestry Room. Hatton Abbey. Rubbing his eyes, he half fell out of bed and felt his way cautiously across the thick carpet to where the window should be.

Unbarring the heavy shutters, he let in a wholly unexpected blaze of sunshine. The clouds had cleared, leaving a broad, brilliant expanse of March blue sky. A spring morning, bringing joy, and a sense of gratitude for the pleasures of being alive.

Life had returned, too, to the gardens below his window. A dark man in a brown apron was clipping one of the yew curlicues at the foot of the steps, while another was trawling dead leaves from the great semi-circular pond. Out in the park, he could see a tractor at work near the far canal. Could that glint of red and green be a woodpecker? In immediate response to his thought came the unmistakable rattle of one drilling busily among the trees by the ruined temple.

There was a knock at his door. 'Nero', with Proby's brown tweed jacket and corduroys, carefully ironed yet still shapeless.

'Will you be wearing this, sir?'

'Thank you, Maurice.' He was getting used to the routine. Nor would he miss the shirt and jeans he'd been lent in the meantime. They had, to be truthful, been shamingly tight, drawing attention to his swelling waistline. For Proby, though not it seemed for Rootham, three square meals a day and no exercise was a luxury he could do without.

'Breakfast will be ready in forty minutes, sir. Shall I run a bath?'

'No, thank you.' There were limits!

Later, leaving his bedroom for the last time, he gazed again at the tall tapestries, Paris choosing beauty, Menelaus with the faithless Helen, Achilles with King Priam weeping over the shattered body of his son Hector, and finally, on the fourth wall, Troy itself, the topless towers of Ilium vanishing in a swirling smoke of *petit point.* Nothing in those dry lessons in Greek mythology with old Mr Morrison at that damp stone school on the edge of Farthingdale more than forty-five years ago had ever prepared him for such delicate beauty.

John Hatton might be in custody, locked with Oates and Allan in the Estate Office overnight, but Sir Thomas seemed more resigned than tearful. As for Hatton Abbey, still this morning showing off the sunlit beauty of its four perfect faces to the world with a sublime indifference as to the imperfections of its owners, as it had done for the last three hundred years? Surely those golden walls would last another three hundred years at least.

Walking down the Gallery towards the great staircase, he met Nanny Fisk, her face as grim as ever, carrying a breakfast tray. The fresh toast smelt delicious.

'For Miss Emily?' he enquired politely.

'I'm not her blooming nursemaid!' growled the old woman in a confiding tone. 'Of course, *she* can twist me round her little finger. Little varmint!' She chuckled, then padded away towards the end of the gallery. In an odd way, he seemed to be becoming accepted as part of the extended family of the house.

Turning left by the portrait of the first Sir Thomas, he began, slowly, to descend. How many other staircases had been built like this? Was it unique? Or was every county, the whole globe for that matter, studded with similar monumental creations? Perhaps he had just led a very protected, and parochial, life, taking it for granted that stairs were no more, nor less, than steps, for getting from one floor to another, instead of like this, statements of pomp and power.

Not that he recoiled from it. On the contrary, he felt himself responding to the exuberance, the soaring imagination and wit that had commissioned, designed and then built such a space, taking a simple need for mobility and transforming it into an essay in splendour.

'Takes a bit of cleaning, this lot.' Even 'Nero' was unbending! True to form, he had crept up to Proby without a sound.

'I should say so.'

'Shall you be leaving after breakfast, sir?'

'Yes. Yes, I will.'

'I'll see that Edward packs your bag.'

'Thank you, Maurice.' Proby had the uneasy feeling that it wasn't that they were getting used to him, but that he was getting used to them.

'The eggs are on the left!' In the dining room, Sir Thomas was tucking in as usual. His height certainly hadn't been determined by any lack of appetite. 'Stinson says the roads are clear now. Just as well. My son Frederick will be coming home today.' He seemed to have forgotten about the three corpses upstairs and his own part in trying to assist his younger son to escape retribution. Although that, no doubt, was the cause of the elder son's abrupt return. 'Stinson says you'd be very ill-advised to take the A690. He says you'd do much better to go round and cross the river at Castlewick and then go home on the southern road.'

Stinson, whoever he might be, thought Proby in a sudden savage reaction against all this stifling security and power, could go to the devil. He just wanted to leave now, to feel Sheila's arms around him again, to get back to real life as he was used to experiencing it. There was a gang of burglars to catch. Protecting *property*? No! He wanted to avenge little Jemima's tears. But then he thought of the little old woman upstairs, tearing off her clothes in her anguish, blundering about in her blindness, being hunted down by her own *son*.

'That's the first time I've seen you show distress, Inspector.' Sir Thomas had caught him off guard. 'I expect you've had enough of us by now.' It was true, but how could he admit it to a man whose son had just been arrested for murdering his mother?

'I was thinking of a little girl who got caught up in a burglary,' he mumbled.

'Do you have any children?'

Proby shook his head. 'No,' he said. 'No, we don't.'

'No doubt you and Mrs Proby regret that. But this weekend may help you to appreciate its consolations.' He said it without the slightest hint of self-pity. 'I felt I had to protect my son. It was my fault. I indulged him too much.' Nothing, it seemed, could really affect the old patriarch. He appeared almost to relish taking on the responsibility for everything and everyone. Perhaps he had been in charge for so long that he could no longer believe that anyone under his roof had the capacity for independent action. No doubt he had conquered his emotions in dealing with his father's disasters. And since then, his pose of invincible stoicism, his apparently imperturbable progress, seeming to drive himself forward through an imperfect world, was, in the end, not a grand exercise in façadism after all, but just the practical reality of a man in his circumstances, in the same way that his ancestor's architect, faced with a dual demand, for symmetry and extra bedrooms, had responded with the transparent trickery of those ambiguous windows. As the house, so the man, the two become one. The fact was, he'd lied without hesitation, about the previous Will, and about his last interview with Boyce.

Proby looked at his host. 'I'm sorry,' he said.

The old man made an indeterminate gesture with one hand. 'Thank you,' he replied, with a flash of that familiar wry smile, a lopsided acknowledgement of reality, 'I know you mean that, which is more than most people would. You thought I was being very foolish when I spoke to you of evil. Yet I think now you would accept that Florence was right. I wish you had known her longer. For someone plagued with extreme ill health she had a rare capacity for insight.' He paused. 'And charm.'

Proby watched him in silence. This man had demanded justice, and had then done his best to pervert it, sending a foolish man to his death in the process. There really was nothing he could say.

'*The Inspector's car is at the door.*' 'Nero', silent as ever, his mouth a scarlet gash across that frozen lifeless face, was standing in the archway.

Proby, thankful to be released, stood up, his breakfast still untouched. 'Goodbye, Sir Thomas.'

The old man rose. 'Goodbye, Inspector. Don't forget to sign the visitor's book in the Library. Maurice will show you where it is.' They shook hands. It was the first time they had touched. The old man's hand was soft and clammy, and he withdrew it swiftly, as if aware of its unpleasant effect.

As Proby returned from signing his name in the thick leather-bound ledger, he passed the foot of the great stairs for the last time. Some infinitesimal sound, magnified by the echoes in that place, a heel scuffed against stone perhaps, caused him to look up. There, silhouetted against the tall window, was that same figure he had seen the first day, Emily, in a pale green dressing-gown, motionless, lit from behind by the yellowish haze of pure light.

Resolutely, he maintained his steady progress, and, seen from above, his upright figure passed out of sight behind a pillar, though the sound of his footsteps continued to beat a rhythmic retreat away towards his own world.

Safe in the police car, Proby settled back against the seat beside Rootham, who, after one look at his face, busied himself with his notebook.

As the car accelerated away, Proby turned round to watch the great honey-coloured house receding into its landscape. The façade of the house was a lie, a monumental exercise in concealing the truth, with all those cramped little rooms piled one above the other behind the tall windows, the most *beautiful* lie he had ever seen.

'Amazing people still live like that,' muttered Rootham. 'All that breakfast'll get thrown away. Edward says they chop it up for the bloody chickens.'

Proby shrugged. He had tried to shake 'Nero' by the hand too, but the butler had just ignored his gesture, staring vacantly out across the busy forecourt, thronged now with official vehicles. Perhaps he had expected to be tipped.

'Any news of those burglars, the *boys-in-blue*?' he asked DC Braithwaite who had driven over to collect them.

'Didn't they tell you, sir? They've had a third go at Barclays. Got away with nearly half a million. PC Bourke's in intensive care. They ran him over in Wynde Street.'

'Bastards!'

'You can say that!' The young man was red in the face with indignation. 'Reversed over him. But he may have clocked one of them. Muttered something about "Jim". DS Henderson's by his bedside, just in case he comes round. He's hoping you'd call.'

'After I've seen my wife.' There'd be time enough to pick up the threads of the case once he'd reassured himself about Sheila first. Back to reality.

Proby lay back in his seat and closed his eyes.